How could she be such a fool?

Why was she allowing Elaine Mendoza to occupy so much of her thoughts? No doubt this was just another ploy on Logan's part to try to frustrate her. He had already admitted to bringing her here under false pretenses. Was his involvement with Elaine intended to be the final humiliation?

Charlotte tossed restlessly on her bed, wishing she could close her ears to the insidious sound of the surf, which was a constant reminder of Logan's nearness. She would have liked to walk again, to fight the tugging wind in her hair and calm herself with the freedom of the elements.

But Logan might be out there on the beach, and more disquieting still, he might not be alone....

ANNE MATHER
is also the author of these

Harlequin Presents

and these

Harlequin Romances

Many of these books are available at your local bookseller.

For a free catalog listing all titles currently available,
send your name and address to:

HARLEQUIN READER SERVICE
1440 South Priest Drive, Tempe, AZ 85281
Canadian address: Stratford, Ontario N5A 6W2

ANNE MATHER

born out of love

Harlequin Books

TORONTO • NEW YORK • LOS ANGELES • LONDON
AMSTERDAM • PARIS • SYDNEY • HAMBURG
STOCKHOLM • ATHENS • TOKYO • MILAN

Harlequin Presents first edition October 1977
ISBN 0-373-10210-0

Second printing October 1977
Third printing October 1977
Fourth printing March 1980
Fifth printing April 1981
Sixth printing August 1982
Seventh printing October 1982
Eighth printing January 1983

Original hardcover edition published in 1977
by Mills & Boon Limited

CHAPTER ONE

CHARLOTTE regarded the bus which was to convey them from the little township of San Cristobal to Avocado Cay with dismay. She had not known such buses existed outside of museums. Jutting bonnet, thick-spoked wheels, wood-framed seats; was the fact that it was painted in a kaleido-scope of colours intended to distract attention from its less favourable attributes?

'Hey, Mum, what a fantastic machine!'

Robert evidently had no such misgivings, and Charlotte turned to her eleven-year-old son with faint resignation. 'Fantastic is right,' she agreed dryly. 'I wonder if the brakes work.'

'Come on, Mum, of course they will.' Robert was opti-mistic. 'These old bangers were built to last.'

'And last and last . . .' declared his mother, smiling her thanks to the dark-skinned West Indian who had hefted their cases out of the launch and into the luggage com-partment of the vehicle which was to transport them the last few miles to their destination, before following Robert's lanky figure up the steps. Tall for his age, and with an appetite which would not have disgraced a weight-lifter, Robert still remained as thin as a lath, she reflected ruefully.

There were few other passengers, fortunately, and at least they were not to be crushed by the press of humanity, Charlotte approved with some relief, subsiding into the seat beside her son. It was just as well. The contours of the bus did not allow for expansion, and although all the windows were open, the air inside was still and humid.

Through the windows, they could see the quay, and the launch which had brought them from Tortola rocking at its mooring. The stones of the quay were bleached white by the sun, which was presently beginning its downward sweep towards the shadowy rise of the densely wooded hinterland, and the water beyond was clear turquoise shading to deepest blue. Whatever else San Cristobal lacked, there was no shortage of colour, Charlotte had, reluctantly, to admit. White-painted buildings, overhung with flowering creepers were dazzling without the protection of dark glasses, and she searched her bag for the polaroid lenses she had bought in St Thomas. A station wagon was coming fast down the narrow road towards the harbour, throwing up a cloud of dust in its passing, drawing attention to the precipitous climb ahead of them, and she hoped Robert was right in his casual assertion that these vehicles were built to last.

Then, realising how tense she was becoming, she forced herself to relax. There was no point in letting the situation play on her nerves. It was too late for that. She was here now; she was committed; and providing Madame Fabergé found her work acceptable, here they would stay.

All the same, it was impossible to rid herself of the bitterness she had felt these past few weeks since Matthew's death. Without it, she might never have considered taking a post in such an out-of-the-way spot, might never have given in to the eagerness to escape from the triumphant condescension of Matthew's relatives. What had they said? That it was only right that he should have left his house and property to his family; his *real* family, that is, not the girl he had taken into his home when she was seven years old, and whom he had had to marry ten years later because she was pregnant with another man's child. The child he had grown to hate ...

Charlotte shivered and looked despairingly at her son. Was this Matthew's way of reaping his revenge, leaving her without even a roof over her head, and only her brief experience of nursery training to fall back on? Had he really lost all feeling for her? Had he allowed his brother and sister-in-law to influence him to that extent?

Of course, she had always known that Malcolm and

Elizabeth had disliked her. They had made that plain in a dozen different ways, not least by forbidding their own two sons to associate with her. As far as they were concerned, Matthew had been mad to take responsibility for her in the first place, and when she had found herself pregnant, she had merely confirmed their opinion of her. But it hadn't been like that ...

She sighed now. How many times during those months before Robert was born had she longed to be able to destroy the child inside her? She hadn't wanted a baby, not *this* baby, and by no means had she wanted to marry a man almost thirty years older than herself.

But Matthew had been adamant. He wanted to care for her, he said, and how could she expect to care for herself? People would talk if she went on living in his house as the mother of a baby, he said. They would suspect it was his, so why shouldn't they convince them of it? Only Malcolm and Elizabeth had known that Matthew was not Robert's father, could *never* have been, and they had never let Charlotte forget it.

In the early days, she used to wonder why a man with money and influence like Matthew Derby should have wanted to take in the orphaned daughter of one of his saleswomen. Those had been innocent days, before she had learned that years ago Matthew had cared for her mother, had wanted her, and had been thwarted when she met and married the young airman who had been Charlotte's father. In those pre-war months Matthew had been an eligible bachelor, elder son of Andrew Derby, who had opened the first of two department stores from which the Derbys had made their money. He had found it incredible that anyone in her mother's position should have preferred a penniless airman to someone with his social advantages, but then the war had overtaken them all, killing Matthew's parents in an air raid and destroying for ever his own hopes of ever fathering a child.

Charlotte had learned the story gradually, through Elizabeth Derby's barbed comments and from the things she

7

had overheard the housekeeper saying. But then she had not really understood the connection between that history and herself. That had come later, and with adolescence came the rude awakening to Matthew's true purpose in putting her in his debt. Even so, she had not taken his advances seriously until her involvement with Robert's father ...

Logan Kennedy had been studying marine biology. His home was in Brazil, but he had come to study for a while at a London institute, and Matthew had met him through a colleague of his at the university. Because Matthew was always interested in something new, he eventually invited Logan to dinner at High Clere, his house in Richmond.

From the beginning, Charlotte had been fascinated by the dark South American. Tall and lean and muscular, with the kind of uneven good looks and deep tan that went with the outdoor life he led, he was totally outside her realm of experience. She was used to spending time with older people, and Logan was much younger than Matthew's circle of friends. Even so, she had never expected him to become interested in her.

Logan only came to High Clere that one time. Whether Matthew sensed he had made a mistake in bringing him there, Charlotte never knew for certain, but what she did soon learn was that Matthew did not approve of her associating with the young Brazilian.

She had left school the previous summer and because she liked children, she had decided to train as a nursery nurse. Brought up without children of her own age, she found working with the toddlers a delight, and that was how Logan had come upon her that afternoon when he had come to the nursery to meet her—with her arms full of children.

To say she had been surprised to see him would have been an enormous understatement. But that had quickly been erased by her very real excitement at his appearance. Because she had been afraid that if she went home and asked Matthew his permission he might refuse, she had

8

telephoned Mrs Parrish, the housekeeper, and explained that she intended having a meal with a friend, and allowed her to draw her own conclusions.

Of course, when she had gone home she had told Matthew the truth, and because he had been surprisingly non-committal she had assumed he had no objections. But she had soon found this was not so. Engagements she couldn't remember accepting were sprung on her at the last minute, forcing her to ring Logan and cancel whatever arrangements they had made. Matthew developed curious aches and pains whenever she was going out, and she found it almost impossible to relax at times, knowing he was sitting at home, waiting patiently for her.

Naturally, Logan began to get impatient. He had so little time in England, and although she began to see what it was Matthew was trying to do, she couldn't help the feelings of guilt he managed to arouse inside her.

Besides which, her relationship with Logan was developing too quickly for her peace of mind. She had had boy-friends before, but never anyone like Logan, and when she was with him she seemed to lose all control over her emotions. She could think lucidly enough when they were apart, but when she was in his arms, sharing kisses and caresses which were all the more passionate because of their brevity, she knew they were rapidly becoming not enough. Sooner or later his own need would break through the iron control Logan kept upon himself, and then ...

Even so, the inevitable might not have happened had it not been for Matthew. Charlotte came home from work one evening in early autumn to find him sunk in a mood of deep depression, seated beside the fire in his study, the bottle and empty glass beside him bearing silent witness to the number of drinks he had already swallowed.

It was then he had broached the subject which in recent weeks she had forgotten—that of the eventual outcome of their relationship. He wanted to marry her, he told her, staring at her through slightly bloodshot eyes, and she had tried to make light of his proposal. But Matthew was not in

9

the mood for levity, and for once in his life he made an entirely uncalculated move. He got up from his chair and jerked her into his arms, pressing his wet mouth to hers. Charlotte could still shudder at the remembrance of that revolting embrace, and she wondered again how she had succeeded in escaping from him. He was a strong man—but he had been drinking, and she fought herself free with all the power of her healthy young body. She went straight to Logan, of course, and there, in his hotel room, in the heat of indignation and the passion which always flared between them, he made love to her.

Afterwards, she had been shocked and tearful, drained of all emotion, and then when Logan would have comforted her, a call had come in from the university and he had gone off to see the principal without even saying goodbye. Charlotte waited, but as time passed she grew cold and frightened, and eventually she returned to High Clere.

The following day Matthew apologised for his behaviour, and ever afterwards she could never remember him imbibing too freely. On the contrary, in the eleven years they were married he seldom took more than a glass of wine with his dinner.

Charlotte waited for Logan to contact her, and when he didn't she rang his hotel, only to be told he had checked out the morning after ... after ...

Time ran together after that. Disillusioned and unhappy, she was horrified when she discovered the results of her recklessness. But Matthew had been surprisingly sympathetic. He rang the university on her behalf and elicited the information that Mr Kennedy had returned to Rio de Janeiro some weeks previously. Charlotte remembered how distraite she had felt not knowing what to do, where to turn, contemplating the possibilities of abortion, all the emotional trauma of an unwanted pregnancy.

Then Matthew had renewed his offer of marriage, with the proviso that she could keep her own room, that things would go on exactly as before. Even so, she had been reluctant to accept. Deep inside her, she had not been able to rid herself of the feeling that perhaps there was some explanation, that perhaps Logan would come back. But he didn't, and as the days and weeks went by, her hopes dwindled and died.

So she married Matthew, as much for his sake as hers, although his family would never accept that. But he had so much more to lose than she did by a scandal, and she knew there was some truth in his assertion that people would suspect that he was responsible.

When Robert was first born, Matthew seemed delighted to have a son, and those early years were happier than even Charlotte could have imagined. But as Robert got older, things changed. Perhaps it was his obvious lack of resemblance to Matthew, or the fact that he got more pleasure out of outdoor pursuits than showing an interest in his father's stores. Or maybe it was simply that like fatigue eating into metal, his brother and sister-in-law's maliciousness got through to him. Whatever it was, Matthew began picking on the boy, chastising him at every opportunity, until Robert himself rebelled and turned on his father.

Until then, Robert had accepted Matthew as his father without inquiry, but suddenly came a spate of questions about how Charlotte came to marry a man so much older than she was, and why when all the other boys at school had young, athletic fathers, his was already an old man.

She parried his questions as best she could, not wanting to make him any more insecure than he already was, but once again it was Matthew who precipitated disaster, throwing his mother's wanton behaviour at him, insinuating that she didn't really know who his father was, destroying for ever any lingering trace of affection Robert might have felt for him.

Whether the bitterness which had corroded his soul was responsible, Charlotte did not know, but two days later Matthew had a heart attack from which he never fully recovered, and six months later he was dead.

Even so she would not have believed he could be so vindictive. The house, the property he owned, all his securities and the interest he had in the Derby stores went to his brother and his family, while Charlotte was left with a little over three hundred pounds in cash, and the small amount of jewellery she possessed.

Naturally, Malcólm and Elizabeth were jubilant. It was nothing less than she deserved, they said, and Charlotte had suffered their taunts in silence. Mr Lewis, Matthew's solicitor, was obviously more sensitive, however, and a few days after the funeral he had come to her with this offer of employment as nursemaid to the small son and daughter of a Madame Fabergé, whose husband was living and working on San Cristobal in the Virgin Islands.

Charlotte had her doubts at first. It was a tremendous step to take, leaving the country to live on a remote Caribbean island with people she had not even met. But Mr Lewis's persuasions and Robert's enthusiasm, allied to her own desire to put both of them out of reach of the influence of Matthew's relatives, eventually swayed the balance. So far, Robert had not questioned her about his real father, but she knew it was only a matter of time before he would want to know. To tell him his father had been a student was not enough, and perhaps, away from England, she could think of some acceptable substitute.

The terms of her employment seemed reasonable: she was to travel out to San Cristobal for a month's trial, at the end of which time both parties would have the option to terminate the contract. Hours of work would be agreed between her employer and herself, and she and Robert would live independently in their own bungalow, a few yards from the Fabergé house. Charlotte had had to admit it sounded ideal, except that Robert would not receive the standard of schooling to which he was accustomed. Before Matthew's death he had been attending a small preparatory school, not far from their home in Richmond, but Charlotte had known that sooner or later she would have to remove him from there. She didn't think Robert would object. He was an easy-going boy, and had the capacity to adapt to circumstances. Which was just as well, she thought wryly.

'Do you think there are sharks out there?'

Robert's eager question diverted Charlotte, and she determined to put all thoughts of Matthew, and the Derbys, out of her mind.

'Well, I expect there are sharks,' she conceded doubtfully, realising this was something else she had not considered. 'But I don't suppose it's dangerous to swim or anything like that.'

'Mmm. Pity,' her son remarked disappointedly, and she gasped. 'Robert!'

'Well...' His grin was rueful, and the memories she had succeeded in stifling moments before came flooding back. Robert's resemblance to his father might not be too obvious yet, but his sense of humour was purely Logan's—that, and his darkness, the sallow cast of his skin after spending too long in northern climes, and the angular leanness of his body which would later acquire the muscular hardness of his father's. 'That would be really something,' he added. 'Seeing a shark!'

'It's something I can do well without,' retorted Charlotte, her tone sharpened by emotion.

'Oh, *Mum*!'

'Besides,' she went on, 'if—and I emphasise the word *if*—you do get the opportunity to go swimming, I shall expect you to remain within your depth.'

'Seventy per cent of shark attacks on bathers occur in two to three feet of water,' Robert observed casually.

'My God!' Charlotte stared at him aghast.

Robert shrugged. 'It's true.'

'Did you have to tell me that?'

His eyes teased hers. 'I thought you'd want to know.'

'Where did you get this information?'

'From an encyclopaedia. When that film *Jaws* was showing, we did this project——'

'Yes, well, I'd rather not know.'

'All right.'

'Oh no—no, that's not true.' Charlotte felt frustrated. How could she explain to her independent son that he meant more to her than anyone else in the world? How could she describe the need she felt to protect him when she knew that Robert would regard her anxiety with typical male impatience of feminine weakness? 'I mean—if that's so, then—you'll have to take care, won't you ...' her voice trailed away.

'I will, Mum. Don't worry.' Robert turned to look out of the window again. 'I say, do you think this is our driver coming now? Gosh, have you ever seen anyone so *fat*?'

'Robert!' Charlotte reproved quietly, although she had to admit he was right. The man approaching the bus must be easily sixteen stones. 'Don't make personal comments.'

But as the man caught hold of the handrail to haul himself aboard, the station wagon Charlotte had noticed earlier, making its descent to the harbour, swung sharply across the sun-bleached stones of the quay and ground to a halt beside him.

Immediately the fat man turned, a broad grin splitting the deeply pigmented lips, and he nodded his head in greeting as the driver of the station wagon thrust open his door and got out. Tall, lean almost to the point of thinness, in close-fitting denim jeans, with roughly cut dark hair overlapping the collar of a faded denim shirt, the man who emerged grasped the hand the fat man extended. They exchanged a few barely audible words, and then they both turned to examine the occupants of the vehicle with close scrutiny.

Charlotte, who had been watching the encounter with only scant interest, suddenly felt her breath catch in her throat, and all the blood drain away from her face. The resemblance between the newcomer and the man who had been occupying her thoughts for the past few minutes was startling. There again was the darkness which had been

14

duplicated in Robert's intelligent features, the lithe economy of movement that reminded her of the sinuous grace of a feline, the detached, appraising stare from eyes which she knew could change, as his emotions changed, from coolest hazel to burning amber.

But she was imagining things, she told herself sickly and without much conviction. She had to be. The man with the undisguisedly cynical expression who was presently survey-·ing the passengers aboard this ancient conveyance could not possibly be the same man who had abandoned her al-most twelve years before, without even troubling to find out whether she had recovered from his assault. It was too great a coincidence. That she should travel half across the world to escape from one situation only to find herself facing something even worse was nothing short of disaster.

Realising she had been holding her breath, she expelled it sharply, unwillingly attracting Robert's attention. He frowned when he saw how pale she had become, and said, with what for him was an unusual show of concern: 'Are you feeling all right, Mum? Your face is all sort of grey-looking. You're not going to pass out or anything, are you?'

Charlotte managed to shake her head. 'I just felt a little dizzy for a minute,' she replied hastily, looking down at her hands, their dampness moulding them together in her lap. 'Just give me a few minutes and I'll be fine.'

Robert was more shrewd than she had given him credit for being. 'Who's that guy who keeps staring at us?' he de-manded in a whisper, bending his head so that no one could read his lips, and Charlotte made the excuse of reproving him for using the Americanism to give herself time to marshal an answer.

'I don't know,' she denied, impatience giving an edge to her tone. 'Robert, stop behaving like a poor imitation of James Bond! He's probably a government official or some-thing, come to check out the hired help.'

Robert lifted his head to return the man's stare, and then

grimaced. 'Blimey,' he gulped. 'he's coming aboard! Did we contravene Customs regulations, do you think?'

Charlotte never failed to be amazed at Robert's grasp of vocabulary. 'Where on earth did you hear that?' she was saying, when the dark man came down the aisle between the rows of seats and stopped beside them.

'Mrs Derby?' he queried politely, and she looked up into Logan's critical gaze.

'Y-yes,' she stammered.

He inclined his head. 'Will you come with me? I'm here to escort you to Avocado Cay.'

Charlotte's mouth was dry. For several seconds she didn't—*couldn't*—say anything, remaining in her seat, staring at him through mists of confusion. It was Logan. She had no doubts about that now. Older, of course—he must be thirty-seven now—with lines etched upon his tanned features which had not been there before, but unmistakably the man who had ravaged her emotions and abandoned her. She ought to feel angry, she thought. She ought to feel resentful and cheated, capable of returning the contempt she could see glinting in those tawny eyes.

Instead, she felt shaken, and apprehensive; terrified of the complications he could create. She glanced anxiously at Robert, half afraid her expression revealed the turmoil in her brain, but he seemed quite relaxed at this unexpected turn of events, obviously just waiting for her to make the first move.

She took a deep breath. What could she do but go with Logan? If Madame Fabergé had asked him to pick them up she had no valid reason to refuse his offer, and certainly Robert would think it strange if she showed a preference for the bus now.

She wondered what Logan was thinking, wishing she could see behind that cool mask he was presenting. Had he decided not to acknowledge her? Were they to behave as if they were the strangers Robert believed? Her heart thumped and she cast another covert look in her son's direction, mentally trying to reassure herself that Logan

16

could never suspect their relationship. Why should he, after all? She had been married, and so far as he was concerned, Robert was the son of that marriage. Yet if he had guessed who she was, why hadn't he made any attempt to stop her from coming here? He must surely have as little desire to see her again as she had to see him.

'Avocado Cay?' she said now, stupidly she realised, and Logan nodded.

'That is where you're going, isn't it?'

'Yes. We're going to Avocado Cay.' Robert spoke up with his usual confidence. 'But Mum's feeling a bit funny, aren't you?' He smiled encouragingly at her before transferring his attention back to the tall man beside them. 'Who're you?'

'Robert——'

Charlotte's hasty reproval went unacknowledged. 'I'm Logan Kennedy,' he answered the boy evenly. 'And as a matter of fact, your mother and I have met before—years ago.' His lips twitched briefly. 'I live at Avocado Cay, too.'

'You do?' Robert pushed back a lock of dark hair, his frown mirroring his confusion. 'But Mum——'

'I expect your mother's forgotten all about our brief encounter,' Logan interposed smoothly. 'I was an—er—associate of your father's.'

'Oh.' Robert looked as though he might be about to say something about that too, but to Charlotte's relief he gave in to other questions: 'What's Avocado Cay like? I can't wait to see where we're going to live. Is there a beach? Will I be able to swim in the sea?'

A faint trace of humour touched Logan's mouth. 'There are miles of beach,' he reassured him. 'And swimming in the sea is possible. But perhaps your mother would prefer you to use the lagoon.'

'The lagoon!' Robert looked intrigued. 'What's that, Mr Kennedy?'

Charlotte made a supreme effort and got to her feet. 'Robert, Mr—Kennedy's not here to answer your questions.' She forced herself to look at Logan. 'I'm ready when

17

you are. Our luggage is stowed somewhere at the back of the bus.'

'I know.' Logan's expression hardened as he looked at her. 'Miguel is presently loading it into my car.'

'Miguel?' Charlotte glanced round in time to see the overweight bus driver closing the rear flap of the station wagon and her lips tightened. 'You were sure we would agree, then?' The words would not be denied.

Logan's heavy-lidded eyes flickered with an emotion she couldn't identify. 'Why not? The journey is rough, whatever the conveyance, and I'd hazard a guess that physically you'll feel safer with me.' He turned. 'Come.'

'Mum wasn't looking forward to riding in this!' agreed Robert, apparently unaware of the undercurrents in their conversation. 'It's a museum piece!'

Following Logan along the aisle to the exit, Charlotte was aware of Robert's voice carrying clearly to the man standing at the foot of the steps, and she wasn't surprised when Miguel pulled a face at him.

'What is this? You are calling my beautiful bus a museum piece!' he exclaimed in mock fury, and Robert grinned widely.

'I'd like to ride with you, Miguel,' he offered placatingly, 'but I don't think Mum could stand the pace!'

Miguel roared with laughter, and Charlotte, prepared to remonstrate with her son once again for his casual use of the man's name, bit her tongue. She saw Logan watching Robert with a curious expression on his face and her heart turned over. What if he should guess the truth? she thought agonisingly, and turned back from the inevitable outcome of such a consequence.

'Perhaps you might prefer to travel in the bus—er—Robert?' suggested Logan quietly, and Charlotte's nerves jangled at the terrifying possibility of having to make the journey to Avocado Cay alone with this man.

But Robert took one look at her pale features and shook his head. 'I don't think so, thanks. Not today anyway. I think I ought to stick with Mum, if you don't mind.'

Logan shrugged and swung open the nearside door of the station wagon. *'De nada,'* he said indifferently, reminding Charlotte that in spite of his perfect English he was not European, and at his silent indication she subsided into the passenger seat with unconcealed relief.

CHAPTER TWO

THE road up from the harbour was little more than a dusty track, that in wet weather might well become dangerous, Charlotte surmised. Within minutes, the harbour had fallen away below them, a natural basin, which from this height revealed light and colour invisible from the quay. As they climbed higher, the air grew fresher, and the wind through the open windows tumbled Charlotte's hair about her shoulders.

The palm groves which fringed the coastline had given way to dense undergrowth which was crushed beneath the wheels of the station wagon where it encroached on to the road. The trees, Charlotte could see, were overgrown with creepers, and their progress sent birds winging into the air, noisily indignant at being disturbed. They could hear water, clear rushing water, that revealed itself in streams and tiny waterfalls tumbling down the mountainside. Ferns and mossy rocks determined its course through pools and cascades, flowering plants clinging to its path for survival.

They followed the curve of a ridge until the harbour was hidden by the shoulder of the island and thick vegetation gave way to waist-high grasses. From here it was possible to glimpse the shapes of other islands in the group, shadowy mounds rising out of the deepening colours of the sea.

Robert, who, like Charlotte, had been silent on the journey up from the quay, now exclaimed eagerly: 'How big is the island?'

'I don't know——' Charlotte was beginning, when Logan interrupted her.

'San Cristobal is approximately twelve kilometres long and seven across at its widest point,' he stated calmly. 'Not very big, as you can see.'

Robert rested his arms along the backs of their seats, obviously regarding this as an invitation for more questions. 'They're volcanic islands, aren't they?'

'Twenty-five million years ago,' agreed Logan dryly.

'Twenty-five million years! Gosh!' Even Robert was impressed by this. 'I can't imagine that—twenty-five million years!'

'Nobody can,' replied Logan, swerving to avoid the protruding buttress of a thickly rooted evergreen. 'But geologically the oldest islands in the Antilles were formed about a hundred and fifty million years ago.'

'Is that so?' Robert frowned. 'Have you made a study of the islands, Mr Kennedy?'

Logan glanced sideways at Charlotte. 'I'm a scientist, Robert. All—*behaviour* interests me.'

Robert was intrigued. 'What kind of a scientist?'

'Oh, Robert, please——' Charlotte glanced round at him, nervously impatient, and then felt dismayed at his obvious lack of comprehension. 'I—Mr Kennedy can't want to answer all these questions!'

'I don't mind.' Logan was infuriatingly casual. 'I'm a marine biologist, Robert. I study underwater life, among other things.'

'How terrific!' Robert was really impressed now. 'Do you go scuba diving—that sort of thing? Like Jacques Cousteau?'

A touch of humour lifted the corners of Logan's mouth. 'Well, I would not put myself in the class of Monsieur Cousteau, but yes—I do spend some of my time underwater. It's a fascinating world.'

'I'd love to see it——' Robert was beginning wistfully, when Charlotte determined that this conversation had gone far enough.

'How well do you know the Fabergés, Mr Kennedy?' she inquired politely, as much from a need to penetrate the wall of isolation she could feel closing around her as a desire to prelude her introduction to her employers.

Logan's long, narrow fingers slid effortlessly round the

21

wheel. 'Quite well,' he replied, after a moment's pause.

Charlotte forced herself to go on. 'I believe Madame Fabergé's husband is working here on the island. Does he work with you, by any chance?'

Logan turned to look at her and for a moment their eyes met and held. But the coldness in his was chilling and she looked away as he answered: 'Madame Fabergé's husband is dead, Mrs Derby. I thought you knew that.'

For a moment, Charlotte's brain spun dizzily. She tried to remember what it was Mr Lewis *had* said, and she could almost swear that he had told her that her employer's husband was living and working at Avocado Cay.

Grasping the frame of the open window for support, she said faintly: 'I didn't know that, Mr Kennedy. How could I?'

Logan shrugged. They had been descending a steep slope for some minutes, and below them stretched the serried ranks of a plantation of some kind. Thick leaves disguised their fruit, but Robert recognised the fleshy green fingers beneath.

'Hey, they're bananas,' he cried excitedly. 'Rows and rows of banana plants!'

Logan gave him an inscrutable smile, his benevolence fading when he again encountered Charlotte's troubled gaze. But he went on to explain that this was the only crop grown in any quantity on the island. They had an unusual amount of rainfall, he explained, and its hilly contours were not suitable for acres of sugar cane. The island was not overly populated either. Apart from the village they could see ahead of them, and Avocado Cay, the small township of San Cristobal was its main settlement.

The village was a thriving community, with weatherboard houses and stores fronting a narrow main street. Charlotte saw the schoolhouse and beside it the Episcopalian church, the churchyard incongruously ordered among such tropical disorder. She wondered how many other white people lived on the island. She had seen mostly black faces.

22

Logan was instantly recognised, and their progress was slowed by his casual exchanges with passers-by. Occasionally, someone would approach the car to take a look at the newcomers, and once a child clung to Logan's open window, cheekily demanding when he was going to be taken sailing again.

'You ought to be in school, Peter,' Logan retorted, smiling to take the edge off the reproof, and in the moments before his features hardened again, Charlotte glimpsed the man who had awakened her to an awareness of her own femininity.

'Will I go to school there?' asked Robert, as the outskirts of the village were left behind, and they passed beneath the hanging branches of a belt of thickly rooted trees.

'That depends,' Logan replied quietly, and Robert, seizing on something else he had heard, went on:

'Do you sail, too? What kind of a boat do you have?'

Charlotte licked her dry lips. 'Perhaps you could explain why you thought I should have known Madame Fabergé's husband was dead,' she suggested tautly, ignoring Robert's impatient sigh.

Logan reached forward and pulled a case of cheroots from the glove compartment, expertly flicking the pack until his lips could fasten round one slender stem and withdraw it. Then he felt in his pocket for a lighter, and applied the flame to its tip before replying.

'Surely the conditions of employment were made clear to you, Mrs Derby,' he said at last.

'Yes.' Charlotte endeavoured to keep the nervous tremor out of her tone. 'I was sent here to take charge of Madame Fabergé's small son and daughter.'

'Philippe and Isabelle. Yes, I know.'

'Then you must also know that I would assume Madame Fabergé had a husband. Why else would she be living in such an—an out-of-the-way place?'

'Is that how you see San Cristobal? As an out-of-the-way place?'

Charlotte sighed. 'Are you denying that, too?'

'I am neither admitting nor denying anything, Mrs Derby,' he returned smoothly.

Charlotte controlled the almost overwhelming desire to scream her frustration at him, and continued carefully: 'You know that San Cristobal is hardly the usual haunt of a widow with two children, Mr Kennedy.'

He frowned. 'No,' he conceded at last, with what she felt was deliberate provocation. 'But don't dismiss these islands too lightly, Mrs Derby. They, like the great rain forests of my own country, make me acutely aware of my own minute contribution to the scheme of things.'

Charlotte breathed a sigh. 'Mr Kennedy, I do not require a lecture on my own insignificance. I accept that. All I wondered was why Madame Fabergé should choose to live here.'

Logan's nostrils flared. 'Pierre Fabergé died of yellow fever six months ago in the Amazon delta!' he stated grimly.

'I'm sorry.' Charlotte moved her shoulders in a gesture of regret. 'I—I gather you knew him.'

'He was my best friend,' replied Logan harshly. 'Lisette —his wife—had no one else.'

Now Charlotte understood. And with understanding came a feeling of withdrawal that had nothing to do with cool common sense. It was easy to see how Mr Lewis had confused the issue. Madame Fabergé's husband had no doubt been a marine biologist, too. That would account for his friendship with Logan. And because of Logan's occupation, it had been assumed that he was her husband.

'You—Madame Fabergé lives with you?' she ventured faintly, and was rewarded by a contemptuous glare.

'Do not judge everybody by your own standards!' he retorted cruelly, and it was fortunate that Robert chose that moment to distract their attention by pointing out the ocean ahead of them.

The road emerged from the trees above dunes of fine coral sand, where creaming waves spread a necklace of white lace. The sand looked pure, and unblemished by

24

human endeavour. Before them lay the calm waters of the lagoon, deepening perhaps to no more than twenty feet, and beyond, maybe a couple of hundred yards out from the shore, the surging waters of the ocean tore themselves to pieces on the barely submerged crenellations of a reef.

'Gosh!' Robert was briefly speechless as he stared at a scene that was straight out of a travelogue, and then he shook his head as he turned to Logan again. 'Is the water warm?'

'Is seventy degrees warm enough for you?'

'Seventy degrees!' Robert hunched his shoulders disbelievingly. 'Man, that's warm!' Then he sat up as signs of habitation signalled their proximity to their destination. 'Where's the lagoon? Is it far from the beach?'

Logan shook his head. 'That's the lagoon, Robert. The calm waters before the reef.'

'Is it? Is it really?' Robert was excited. 'But why is it called a lagoon? I thought that was a lake or something.'

Logan hesitated. 'Without the protection of the reef, these waters would be accessible to the biggest and most dangerous fish in the Caribbean.'

'Sharks!' said Robert, not without some satisfaction, and Charlotte shivered.

'Yes. Sharks,' agreed Logan flatly. 'But barracuda, too.'

'Have you ever tangled with a shark, Mr Kennedy?' Robert asked eagerly, and Charlotte saw Logan's mouth turn downward at the corners.

'There are many types of shark, Robert,' he told the boy quietly. 'And not all of them are dangerous. The largest fish in the sea is a whale shark, and it's quite harmless.' He cast a strange look in Charlotte's direction. 'But some sharks—like some women—are unpredictable, and until you learn to recognise the species, you should leave them alone.'

Avocado Cay was a collection of dwellings bordering the ocean. Here and there, attempts at cultivating gardens had been made, but the rioting undergrowth and off-shore winds had almost defeated them. They were verandahed

25

buildings, mostly, with corrugated roofs, set in clearings between flowering shrubs and ubiquitous palms. A few goats grazed on the outskirts of the village, and hens scattered before the wheels of the station wagon. They could smell the sea, its sharp salty tang coming strongly through the windows of the vehicle. The clarity of the air was startling, and only the blown spume on the reef misted the distant horizon.

Logan drove through the village, following a narrow track which led down through a belt of palms and eucalyptus trees almost to the water's edge. Ahead of them, Charlotte could see the roofs of several single-storied buildings, and beyond, a wooden landing jutting out into the lagoon where a sailing ketch was moored. It all looked very beautiful and very peaceful, and without the presence of the man beside her, she would have felt a greater sense of relief.

'Is this where we're going to live?' demanded Robert, voicing the question which had trembled on his mother's lips, and Logan nodded.

'Yes. That bungalow directly ahead of us belongs to Madame Fabergé.'

'And where is our house?' Robert persisted, but Charlotte again intervened.

'I expect—Madame Fabergé will explain where we're going to stay, Robert,' she told him quellingly, avoiding looking at the man beside her. Then: 'Now what are you doing?'

Robert grinned. 'Taking off my sandals. I can't wait to try the water.'

'Robert! At least let's meet my employer first.'

Logan slowed the station wagon as they neared the sand-strewn slope beside the bungalow. 'Didn't I explain?' he asked with deliberate irony: 'You already did—meet your employer, I mean. I employed you, Mrs Derby. Didn't I make that clear?'

Charlotte's lips trembled, and she pressed them together to hide the fact before gasping distractedly: 'You know you didn't!'

Logan's thick lashes shaded his eyes, but his expression was unmistakably smug. 'Well, I'm sorry, but I am. Does it make any difference?'

Charlotte's breathing felt constricted. 'You—you——' she began chokingly, and then became aware of Robert's startled eyes watching her. Pressing a hand to her throat, she moved her head in a helpless gesture of defeat, and the station wagon slowed to a halt as a small boy came darting round from the back of the building to meet them. The child's face was tear-stained, and his tee-shirt and shorts were grubby with sand.

'Uncle Logan! Uncle Logan!' he yelled excitedly, and Logan swung out of the vehicle to catch the small figure up in his arms.

'Olà, Philippe!' he exclaimed, one long finger tracing the marks of tears on his cheek. 'What have you been doing now?'

'Nothing.' Philippe looked sulky for a moment, and then his attention was attracted by Robert getting out of the back of the station wagon. 'Who's that?'

'That's Robert,' answered Logan easily, turning towards the older boy. 'Perhaps he might be persuaded to play with you sometimes. Providing you remember you are only four years old.'

Robert grinned. 'Hi, Philippe,' he said, somewhat self-consciously. 'How are you?'

Philippe wriggled down from Logan's arms, surveying the newcomer's five feet from half that height, and Charlotte deemed it time she made her presence apparent. She pushed open her door and got out just as a plump woman of medium height came down the verandah steps to join them.

It was reasonable to assume that this was Lisette Fabergé. She was carrying a baby of perhaps nine months, a fat little thing wearing nothing but a nappy, and she was obviously in some distress. Her dishevelled appearance matched the dishevelled appearance of her son.

'Oh, Logan, thank goodness you're back!' she exclaimed, with evident relief, ignoring Charlotte standing beside the car and going straight to the man.

Logan turned towards her, sparing a smile for the baby before his concern made itself apparent. Tall and masculine, he dwarfed Lisette, and Charlotte felt an ugly feeling of resentment stirring inside her. So much solicitude for Lisette Fabergé's widowed state, while she had had to cope alone with the fears of her unwanted pregnancy! Watching Lisette's fingers curving possessively round the muscular flesh of his forearm, her eyes turned up to him in appeal, made her feel physically sick, and she slammed the car door with unwarranted force.

Immediately Lisette's wide blue eyes switched in her direction, appraising her and dismissing her in one scornful stare. She was an attractive girl, somewhere around her own age, Charlotte guessed, but there the resemblance ended. For years Charlotte had been accustomed to dressing in styles suitable to the wife of a man with Matthew's money while Lisette's clothes were stained and unpressed and obviously cheap. She was not at all the chic Frenchwoman Charlotte had expected.

'Oh, hello,' she said indifferently, and Charlotte realised she was not French at all, but English. Then she turned back to Logan. 'Phil swallowed one of Isabelle's safety-pins just after you'd left, and I've been frantic!'

'Was it open?' asked Logan at once, a fleeting trace of resignation crossing his face.

'I don't know,' cried Lisette, and Philippe started to cry again.

Logan crouched down beside the boy. 'Now stop that,' he said gently. 'You must know whether the pin was open or not.'

Philippe sniffed. 'It wasn't.'

'You're sure about that?' Philippe nodded, and Logan straightened again. 'So where's the problem?'

Lisette's jaw trembled. 'He didn't tell me that!'

'Didn't he?'

'No. He just ran away when I tried to catch him, and

28

Isabelle was screaming for her tea, and——'

'—and you shouted at him and frightened him,' finished Logan patiently. 'I know.'

'Oh, Logan, you're so *good* with him!'

Charlotte turned away to stare across the stretch of sand to the water's edge. Dear God, was there no end to her punishment? she wondered bitterly. Eleven years of living with a man she did not love should have been enough for anyone.

Fortunately, Robert was unaware of her feelings. His own thoughts lay in an entirely different direction, and it only took Philippe's tentative indication towards the ocean to send them both charging across the sand to the water's edge. Charlotte opened her mouth to call her son, and then closed it again when Logan spoke.

'This is Mrs Derby, Lisette,' he said. 'I'm sure you'll find her assistance a great help with the children.'

Charlotte turned reluctantly and approached them. Isabelle was wriggling impatiently in her mother's arms, and glad of anything to divert her awareness of Logan's penetrating gaze, she held out her arms towards the baby. Isabelle hesitated only a moment before returning the invitation, and with a shrug Lisette dumped the child on to her. Isabelle was wet, among other things, but Charlotte had never liked the cream silk dress she was wearing, and decided ruefully that at least now she had a reason for getting rid of it. She knew Logan was watching her with guarded eyes, but now she felt less vulnerable.

'I can't imagine why a woman like you would want to come out here,' remarked Lisette by way of an opening, obviously as aware of the differences between them as Charlotte was. She was looking down at her own grubby shirt and pants with dislike, clearly favouring the dress Charlotte was so willing to discard.

'Needs must,' Charlotte said now, deciding to be honest about that at least.

'Really?' Lisette looked sceptical. 'I would have thought a job was the last thing you'd need.'

'Appearances can be deceptive,' replied Charlotte, more easily, pulling Isabelle's sticky fingers out of her hair. Then, realising something more was expected of her, she added: 'What a beautiful place this is!'

'It's all right.' Lisette looked reflectively at Logan. 'Are you coming in?'

Logan shook his head. 'Not right now. I think I should show—Mrs Derby where she and her son are going to sleep.'

'That's your son?' Lisette asked Charlotte thoughtfully. 'You must have been very young when he was born.'

Charlotte could do without questions like that. Equally, she could do without Logan showing her where she was going to sleep. 'I—if there's anything you would like me to do now——' she began hastily, only to be silenced by the look Logan cast in her direction.

'Well——' Lisette started, but Logan broke in flatly: 'Not tonight, Lisette. Mrs Derby's had a long day. I think something to eat, a bath, and an early night is indicated, don't you?'

Lisette shrugged, half sulkily, looking very like Philippe had done earlier. 'What shall I give her to eat?'

'I had Carlos take the liberty of providing Mrs Derby and her son with a ready-made meal earlier in the day,' Logan stated evenly. 'Relax, Lisette. Everything's been taken care of.'

'Except Philippe.'

'What about Philippe?'

'Have you forgotten the pin?'

'No, I haven't forgotten,' Logan told her tolerantly. 'The pin will make its reappearance, don't worry. Just keep your eyes open for the next couple of days.'

Lisette pursed her lips and turned back to Charlotte, clearly not altogether suited by his proposal. 'You'd better give Isabelle to me before she ruins your dress completely,' she said, half sullenly.

'It will wash,' Charlotte reassured her, handing the child over with faint regret, and Lisette uttered an angry imprecation as Isabelle began to protest noisily.

'Everything around here has to,' she stated shortly, and marched back up the steps and into the bungalow, leaving Charlotte to face Logan alone.

He seemed rather preoccupied just then, his eyes intent on the two boys splashing in the shallows along the shoreline. Looking at him unobserved, Charlotte felt something uncurl and expand inside her, something that sent the blood more thickly along her veins and probed without sensitivity at her inflamed emotions. He was still the only man she had ever known to exude that aura of raw masculinity, and whether it was in a lounge suit or the revealing jeans he was presently wearing, the way he moved aroused feelings she had long forgotten. Had they really once been *that* close to one another? she asked herself incredulously. Had she lain beside him and ached for his possession, run her fingers over the smooth brown skin of his body and exulted in the trembling passion he had found impossible to control in her arms? Moisture prickled all along her spine, even though the air was much cooler now as the sun sank lower. Oh God, she thought wretchedly, it was more than eleven years ago. She must not think of *that* now!

Then Logan turned and encountered her eyes upon him, and his expression banished all traces of tremulous emotion. 'Come with me!' he commanded harshly, and she followed him obediently down the dusty slope to where a second bungalow was situated in the shade of a clump of gnarled coconut palms.

Shallow steps led up to a verandah, which ran right round the house and would no doubt give access to the beach from the other side, but Logan threw open the door leading into the living room, and Charlotte had, perforce, to follow him inside. He stood in the middle of the sparsely furnished room, with its chintzy upholstery and rug-strewn floor, a darkly malevolent accuser, and when the fugitive wind slammed the door behind her, she knew that the moment of truth had come.

'Well, Charlotte,' he said coldly, and she had to steel

herself not to show her fear of him. 'It's been a long time.'

'Yes.' The word came out squeakily higher than was normal, and she cleared her throat nervously.

'You've changed,' he went on critically. 'You used not to be so sophisticated.'

'I'm older, Logan,' she answered, achieving a coolness she was far from feeling. 'You—you've changed, too.'

'Have I?' His lips curled. 'You married Derby.' It was almost an accusation.

'Yes.' Again the single word stuck in her throat.

'Why?'

'*Why?*' Charlotte stared at him lamely, reduced in a moment to trepidation again.

'Yes, why?' Logan demanded grimly. 'A simple enough question, I should have thought.'

He would have thought ... Charlotte's teeth clattered together. If he only knew! But he mustn't—he *shouldn't*. She licked her dry lips. 'Why do two people usually marry?' she ventured faintly, and was shocked by the reaction this evoked.

'Don't pretend to me that you married Derby because there was any trace of emotion between you?' he snarled savagely, coming close to her so that his breath was a searing draught of air against her forehead. She was a tall girl, five feet seven in her stockinged feet, but Logan had always towered over her. He did so now, the hard muscles of his legs almost brushing her skirt. 'I was there, remember,' he added. 'I know how you regarded him, and it wasn't in *that* way!'

'Cir—circumstances—can alter cases,' she began, but his angry imprecation silenced her.

'Sure they can,' he agreed contemptuously. 'Particularly if the circumstances are governed by those pretty little pieces of paper with green backs!'

Charlotte gasped indignantly. 'Are—are you implying that I—I married Matthew for his money?'

Logan's lips twisted. 'No, I'm not implying it, Charlotte.

I'm *stating* it! What a pity the old man found out too soon and changed his will!'

Charlotte's reaction was swift and instinctive. If she had stopped to consider what she was about to do, she might never have done it. But she didn't think. Her hand moved almost of its own volition, connecting with Logan's cheek with stinging accuracy.

For a moment he stared at her, his hand raised almost disbelievingly to the injury. And then he reacted as she had done, ruthlessly delivering a painful slap to the side of her face.

'*Mum!*'

The door to the bungalow had opened without their becoming aware of it, and now Robert stood motionless in the doorway, staring at them through dazed, accusing eyes.

At once Logan turned aside from Charlotte, raking back his hair much as Robert himself might have done, confronting the boy with evident regret.

'I'm sorry you had to see that, son,' he said wearily, and her heart plunged at his casual use of the word that to him had no meaning. He glanced round at Charlotte, but she avoided his gaze, her eyes watering from the blow on her cheek. 'Your mother and I—well, we had some unfinished business——'

Charlotte had thought Robert's immobility was due to fear or apprehension, but now she realised how wrong she had been. He was pale, it was true, but with anger, not alarm. Gathering his forces, he charged at the man who had so abused his mother, kicking and punching at him with all the wiry strength he possessed.

Logan held him at bay without too much difficulty, but still Robert managed to kick out with his bare feet, and quickly Charlotte intervened. 'Robert!' she cried, grasping his arm and trying to drag him away from Logan. 'It's all right. It's all right! Please—stop this before someone gets hurt!'

It was difficult, but eventually she separated them, shaking Robert gently, forgetting her own pain, both mental and physical, in an attempt to reassure the boy. 'Listen to me,' she exclaimed, forcing him to look at her. 'You don't understand ...'

'I don't want to!' retorted Robert, half tearfully now, as emotion got the better of valour. His lips trembled. 'If I was older, he wouldn't dare to touch you!'

'That's true,' agreed Logan heavily, behind him. 'I wouldn't. I'm sorry, Robert. I promise you, it won't happen again.'

The boy tore himself away from his mother and faced the man fearlessly. Watching them, Charlotte was appalled at how alike they were. 'You bet it won't!' he muttered childishly, and Logan's eyes sought and found hers above her son's head.

'I'll show you the rest of the bungalow,' he said, in a curiously flat voice, but Charlotte declined.

Drawing herself up to her full height, which in cork-soled sandals was a couple of inches more, she said: 'We can manage, thank you. We shan't need your assistance.'

Logan inclined his head wearily. 'As you wish.' He turned towards the door, and she wondered why her victory suddenly felt so much like defeat. 'There are provisions in the kitchen, and the meal my man, Carlos, prepared for you earlier is in the refrigerator. The sanitary arrangements are, I think, self-explanatory.' He paused, one hand on the lintel. 'Carlos will fetch your cases from the car, and I will see you both in the morning.'

Charlotte nodded, but Robert muttered: 'Not if we see you first!' in a distinctly audible undertone.

Logan's look narrowed. 'If you need—anything else, my house is just a dozen yards away along the beach,' he added quietly, and stepped through the door. 'Goodnight.'

Robert turned his back and said nothing, but Charlotte acknowledged his farewell with a quick nod, going to the door as he crossed the verandah, and closing it securely behind him. There was a key and she turned it, uncaring whether or not he heard her.

CHAPTER THREE

It was the sea that awakened her, the persistent sound of the surf breaking on the jaws of the reef a hundred yards away. It was not an unpleasing sound, but it was sufficiently unusual to someone used to the sounds of traffic to disturb the light slumber she had fallen into just before dawn. She lifted her wrist reluctantly, and the broad square face of the masculine watch she wore swam into focus. Six-thirty, she read resignedly. Still too early to get up really, and besides, was she in such a hurry to start the day?

Sun was filtering through the window shutters, dust motes floating in the shafts of light it created. They settled on the square oak dressing table and matching chest of drawers, and on the heavy carved doors of the wardrobe. Apart from these items, and the amply proportioned bed, there wasn't much else in the room, and the night before she had done no more than unpack Robert's pyjamas and her nightgown after Carlos had delivered their cases. Not that sleeping attire was absolutely essential, she thought wryly. She had spent the night on the top of the covers, but without her cotton nightgown she might well have found some use for the quilt beneath her.

With a sigh, she sat up and swung her feet to the floor, her toes curling into the woolly rug beside the bed. Immediately her reflection was thrown back at her from the long, if somewhat pitted, mirrors on the wardrobe doors, and she pulled a face at herself as she rose to her feet. The streaked honey-brown hair, which during the day she wore either in a chignon or coiled on top of her head, tumbled about her shoulders from its centre parting. Matthew used to tell her the styles she wore gave her features a Madonna-like innocence, but she wondered what Logan would say to that. She had worn her hair loose in the days when she had known him, and although she was unaware of the fact, with her hair loose about her shoulders, she looked very little older now than she had done then. Life had left her curiously untouched by experience, and her brief affair with Logan had been overshadowed until now by the presence of the child.

Charlotte sighed again, lifting her arms and holding the heavy hair up from her neck. The action lifted her breasts, too, and their pointed fullness was outlined against the thin cotton of her nightgown. For a moment she had a sensuous, wanton beauty, and then she dropped her arms again and turned abruptly away, embarrassed by the intimate trend of her thoughts. Throughout her marriage to Matthew, she had avoided any reminder of what the relationship between a man and a woman could be, but it was impossible to consider the events of the day before without remembering her relationship with Logan, and speculating on what might have been.

She padded across to the window, and thrusting open the shutters gazed out on the vista of sea and sand that awaited her. The sky was translucent, feathered with clouds that had the opacity of mother-of-pearl, the horizon misty gold and indistinct. Nearer at hand, sand crabs scuttled sideways towards the water, and overhead a hawk hung motionless before dropping like a stone to trap its prey. It was a familiar yet an alien world, possessing so much that she understood, and so much that she did not.

She thought unhappily about the previous evening. It had not been a comfortable few hours. After Logan's departure, Robert had become silent and morose, and she had known he naturally resented the possibility that there might be something else going on about which he knew nothing. It awakened all her fears about him asking about his real father, and her facile explanation that Logan and Matthew had disliked one another had sounded feeble even to her ears. Robert was nobody's fool, and in consequence he had shown little interest in the rest of the bungalow, and eaten

36

sparingly of the delicious chicken salad she had found in the refrigerator.

But how could she explain her relationship to Logan Kennedy without either telling the truth, which was unthinkable, or involving herself in a tissue of lies and evasions? And why did Logan despise her so for marrying Matthew? What was it to him, after all? Surely she was the one who had most to feel resentful about. Her fingers probed the still tender skin of her cheek, where his hand had connected, and she shivered. The Logan she remembered had not been so ruthless. On the contrary, the strength he had possessed had been tempered with gentleness, a quality of which Charlotte had known little in her lifetime.

Which brought her to another point: if Logan had known who she was before she came to San Cristobal, why hadn't he stopped her from coming? It didn't make sense, and the knowledge that she was obliged to spend four weeks on the island before terminating her contract filled her with alarm. Her relationship with Robert had always been so good. Yet now she was in a position to put that relationship in jeopardy—in more ways than one . . .

Heaving a sigh, she turned away from the window, surveying the room behind her with troubled eyes. There was still Lisette Fabergé to consider. Exactly what was *her* relationship with Logan? It was all very well for him to explain that her husband was dead and that she had no one else, but where did they go from there? And when it was obvious that she turned to him for guidance in everything, wasn't it reasonable to assume that sooner or later he would marry her?

Charlotte's nerve-endings tightened. It didn't matter to her what Logan Kennedy should choose to do, she told herself angrily. He had walked out on her eleven years ago, and just because now he was showing masculine hostility at the knowledge that she had quickly found someone else to replace him, there was no reason for her to get involved. But she was involved, a small voice inside her taunted stubbornly. Nevertheless somehow she had to persuade Robert that in spite of their eventful arrival, ultimately the situation was as expected. How ludicrous that sounded, she thought bitterly, realising it would take more than her reassurance to convince her son.

The sound of metal falling on to rubber tiles alerted her to the fact that in spite of the early hour, Robert was already about. Without stopping to dress, she stepped into her mules, and opened the bedroom door. Robert's bedroom, which was across the hall from her own, was empty, and she padded along the passage to find him.

The kitchen door stood wide and the kettle was almost boiling. Robert, in blue cotton pyjama trousers, was busily setting cups and saucers on a tray, and guessing he meant to surprise her, Charlotte would have drawn back. But the sound of her mules attracted his attention, and he spun round to face her, a slightly shamefaced expression marring his lean features. His black hair flopped untidily over his forehead, and as he lifted his hand to push it back, she could see all the bones of his rib-cage through his pale skin.

'I—er—I was just making some tea,' he offered, gesturing towards the tray. 'Did you—did you sleep well?'

Charlotte moved into the room, glancing round casually at the colour-washed walls and steel units. 'Did you?' she countered gently, and he pushed his jaw forward childishly.

'Not very,' he mumbled, and then, as the kettle boiled, turned away to make the tea. When the teapot was sitting squarely on the tray beside the cream jug and sugar basin, he added, in a muffled tone: 'I wish we'd never come here!'

Charlotte sighed, and came round the table which stood in the middle of the floor to get close to him. 'Do you, Robert?' she asked softly. 'Do you really?'

He looked up at her miserably. 'I didn't—not at first. I was looking forward to it. All the boys back home said they wished they could come and live in the West Indies, and yesterday morning, when we sailed from Tortola, it was super! It really was.'

'Then?'

'That man—Kennedy. He spoilt it.'

Charlotte found herself compelled to ask: 'Don't you like him?'

Robert shrugged his bony shoulders. 'I did—to begin with. I mean,' he went on, as if to justify himself, 'his job is jolly interesting, isn't it? And he knows such a lot about the islands—everything. I was looking forward to talking to him some more—maybe even learning about underwater biology and diving.'

Charlotte shook her head, but she found she could not allow Logan's son to dismiss his father out of hand. 'Listen, love,' she said, looking down at him, her hands resting lightly on his shoulders, 'nothing has changed. Not so far as you are concerned——'

'Yes, it has!'

'No!' She squeezed his shoulders more tightly. 'Robert, what you saw—what you shouldn't have seen—yesterday has nothing to do with you. What's between—Mr Kennedy and me has no bearing on your relationship with him.'

'Of course it does.'

'Why?'

Robert stared at her. 'You're my mother. No one's going to hit you while I'm around and get away with it.'

'Oh, love ...' Charlotte felt a ridiculous lump come into her throat, and for once he made no protest when she hugged him. Then she drew back and looked at him again. 'Robert, you must try to be realistic. Ours is an adult world, and some things can't be explained. But believe me when I say you shouldn't prejudge a situation.'

'You mean, you deserved his slapping you?'

'Well, I slapped him first,' admitted Charlotte reluctantly.

'You did?' Robert uttered a boyish whoop. 'Hell, I'd like to have seen that!'

Charlotte shifted impatiently. 'Maybe you would, but

I'd be glad if you'd moderate your language.'

'Oh, Mum, everybody says *hell* these days!'

'Do they?'

'Sure.'

'Americanisms, too, I suppose.'

Robert grinned, and a surge of relief swept over her at the knowledge that he didn't appear to blame her, at least. 'Where shall we have the tea?' he asked, and she suggested they went into her bedroom as they had been accustomed to doing at High Clere.

Sitting cross-legged on her bed, however, Robert returned to the subject she most wanted to avoid. 'How long is it since you've seen Mr Kennedy?' he asked curiously.

Charlotte was glad of her teacup to disguise her expression, but she determined to get this over with, once and for all. 'I—er—met him several years ago, in England,' she replied slowly. 'I told you that.' She paused. 'He and your father——'

'Matthew Derby was not my father!'

'No. Well, as I was saying, they—they met through Matthew's connections with the university.'

'And he came to our—to High Clere?'

'Yes.'

'Did I meet him?'

Charlotte cleared her throat. 'No.'

'Why not?'

'Well, I—I expect you were in bed,' she responded hastily, and despised herself for getting into this position. Finishing her tea, she slid off the bed, and walked across to the windows. 'It's a beautiful morning, isn't it?'

There was silence for so long that eventually she had to turn and look at him, finding him watching her with curiously speculative eyes. Then he smiled, and the momentary chill she had experienced disappeared again.

'Shall I start school straight away?' he asked unexpectedly, and the simply question created another problem.

'I—don't know,' she conceded, her dark brows ascending. 'That's one of the things we'll have to find out.'

'At home, the schools will soon be closing down for the summer holidays,' Robert reminded her hopefully. 'There doesn't seem much point in starting something I'm not going to finish.'

'What do you mean?'

'Will we be staying here after your probationary month is up?' he explained.

Charlotte could feel the warm colour invading her cheeks. 'What makes you ask that question?'

'I don't know,' Robert shrugged. 'Just last night—well, I heard you moving about in here long after we went to bed.'

Charlotte sighed. 'As I haven't even begun working for Madame Fabergé yet, how can I tell?' she lied unhappily, and wished for once that Robert was no more than Philippe's age, and therefore less apt to jump to the right conclusions. 'Now, I think you'd better go. I want to get dressed.'

Robert got obediently off the bed and regarded her with narrow-eyed appraisal. 'Are you going to tie up your hair?'

Charlotte spread her hands. 'Does it matter?'

Robert shrugged, hauling up the pyjamas that hung loosely on his hips. 'Just, I was thinking—well, you're about the same age as Philippe's mother, aren't you?'

'Yes.' Charlotte wondered what was coming next.

'So I just thought that perhaps now that—that *he's* dead, you might wear your hair loose for a change.'

'In this climate? I think not.'

'You look nicer with it loose. Younger.'

'Yes. Well, being nursemaid to Philippe and Isabelle requires me to be efficient, that's all, not glamorous,' she declared tersely, and Robert made a conciliatory gesture as he went out of the room.

All the same, after she had bathed and made her bed, she did look long and critically at her hair before coiling it into the smooth chignon which curved back from her cheeks, concealing her ears, and resting neatly against the nape of her neck.

Clothes presented another problem. Somehow, she didn't think Lisette Fabergé would expect her to wear a uniform, but on the other hand, she could hardly appear in another of the expensive models Matthew had bought her. She rummaged in her cases, discarding item after item, and eventually brought out a pair of purple cotton jeans and a matching shirt. They were not new. She had bought them a couple of years ago. But fortunately her figure had changed little, and apart from a slight shrinkage in the pants which made them rather tighter than she would have liked, they looked serviceable.

Robert, however, made her think differently when she appeared to prepare breakfast. 'That's better!' he approved admiringly, prowling round her. 'I always said you should wear trousers more often.'

Charlotte made an impatient gesture. 'They're working clothes, that's all,' she declared shortly. 'Now what do you want to eat? There seems to be plenty of fruit. Do you want to try mango?'

They were seated at the kitchen table finishing their meal with toasted rolls and grapefruit marmalade when someone knocked at the verandah door. At once Charlotte's tension returned, but when Robert went to answer it, she expelled her breath on a sigh when she saw the tall black man waiting outside.

'Oh—good morning, Carlos,' she called, putting down her coffee cup. 'Come in.'

The black man was carrying a basket, and even before he put a foot over the threshold she could smell the delicious aroma of warm bread. 'Mr Logan, he said you might like some fresh rolls, ma'am,' he explained, setting the basket down on the table and drawing back the napkin to reveal the crusty brown *croissants*. 'But it seems like you've had your breakfast.'

Charlotte looked up at him apologetically. 'We were both awake early,' she explained smilingly. 'But thank Mr—Logan—just the same. I toasted a couple of the rolls we had left from yesterday, and you'd provided us with plenty of fruit.' She paused. 'Oh, and by the way, thank you for the salad. It was delicious.'

Carlos looked unconcerned. 'Glad you liked it, ma'am.' His eyes flickered over Robert, who was standing near the open doorway. 'I'll leave the rolls anyway. You might like them later.'

'Thank you.'

Carlos hesitated. 'Mr Logan also said to ask you whether you'd prefer me to prepare your meals for you. I mean, naturally, I'll keep your cold store stocked in any case, but it would save you——'

'Oh, I don't think that's necessary, thank you, Carlos.' Charlotte rose to her feet now, shaking her head. 'It's kind of you to offer, but I think Robert and I can manage.'

'Mr Logan seemed to think you wouldn't be much used to making your own meals, ma'am,' Carlos added, with an unexpected lack of tact, and she could feel her spine stiffening.

'Mr Logan doesn't know me very well, Carlos,' she replied tartly, and the black man shrugged his bulky shoulders indifferently.

'No, ma'am,' he agreed, and moved towards the door.

'Carlos!'

Her impulsive summons made him turn again. 'Yes, ma'am.'

Charlotte bit her lip. 'I—have you known Mr Logan long?'

She could feel Robert's eyes on her, and was relieved when Carlos's bulk came between them. 'Fifteen years, ma'am.'

'Fifteen years? That's a long time.'

'Yes, ma'am.'

Charlotte nodded, and he took her silence as dismissal. So, she thought ruefully, he had known Logan before she did. How much did he know of their previous relationship? How much might Robert inadvertently hear from him?

Robert left the door open and came back to the table to finish his orange juice. 'The men are big around here, aren't they?' he commented, wiping his mouth with the back of his hand, and then grimacing at his mother's expression. 'First Mr Kennedy, then Carlos. Are all West Indians tall?'

'He's not a West Indian,' said Charlotte unthinkingly. 'He's Brazilian. They both are, I should think.'

'South Americans!' murmured Robert thoughtfully. 'Hmm, that explains it.'

'Explains what?' Charlotte was not really in the mood for his chatter.

'Why they're so big. I read once that the bigger the continent, the bigger the men. You know—room to expand, that sort of thing.'

'Oh, Robert!' Charlotte gathered their dirty dishes together and carried them to the sink. 'You can't generalise like that.'

He shrugged, and picked up a tea towel. 'Why not? That's how statistics are reached. Through generalisations. Mr Hendry was telling us——'

'Well, I'm sure there's more to it than that,' retorted Charlotte, with asperity, and then felt contrite when he hunched his shoulders and shut up.

It was still only eight-thirty when Charlotte left the bungalow to walk the few yards to the Fabergé house. She had left Robert sitting moodily on the steps of the verandah, kicking his toes in the sand, under orders not to swim out of his depth without supervision. This instruction had created some argument, and with the memory of the previous evening's unpleasantness still hanging over her head, Charlotte wished she had not had to be so firm. But it was no good. She would never have any peace if she was worrying about him, and she owed it to Lisette Fabergé to give her whole attention to her job. Perhaps later on in the morning, she might bring the two younger children down to the beach, thus giving Robert his chance to swim where he pleased.

As she walked up the slope, Charlotte saw Logan's house. It was a single-storey beach house, standing on cross supports at the edge of the dunes, with a wooden walkway leading down from it to the landing. She couldn't see Logan, but the station wagon was parked to one side, its bonnet open, and only the rear half of Carlos's body could be seen as he tinkered about inside. He was far enough away from her not to be able to hear what she was doing, and the peaceful scene was somehow reassuring.

Mounting the steps, she knocked at Lisette Fabergé's door. There was no sign of life, and now that she came to notice it, the shutters were still closed at the windows. Frowning, she tried the door, but it was locked, and she shifted her weight restlessly from one foot to the other, wondering what she ought to do now. Surely Lisette was up. Perhaps she had already gone out. But somehow that didn't seem so likely.

She was hovering there uncertainly, hands pushed into the seat pockets of her jeans, when she saw Logan walking up the slope towards her. This morning he was wearing nothing but a pair of fraying denim shorts, and she could see the fine dark hair that partially obscured the brown expanse of his chest. The hair ran down in a vee to his navel, and she looked down deliberately at the open toes of her sandals, aware that staring could be too revealing.

'Good morning,' he said, halting below her, one bare foot raised to rest on the verandah steps, his eyes coolly assessing her. 'Did you sleep well?'

Charlotte saw no reason to lie to him. 'Not very,' she conceded shortly, noticing the shadow of the unshaven chin. Then: 'Do you know where Madame Fabergé is?'

'As I haven't spent the night with her, I can't be sure, but I'd hazard a guess that she was still in bed,' he remarked insolently. 'Would you like me to find out?'

Charlotte took a deep breath. 'She can't still be in bed! Not with two young children! The baby——'

'Lisette doesn't sleep very well,' Logan retorted, straightening and flexing his shoulder muscles. 'As for Isabelle, no doubt she'll be putting up a protest any time now.'

'But Philippe!'

'I don't expect that young man's still in bed. He's probably up and out by now. He spends a lot of his time with the doctor's children up the road.'

'You have a doctor here?' Charlotte coloured at his interrogative stare. 'I mean—I didn't know.'

'No, you didn't,' he agreed dryly. 'So? What do you want me to do?'

'You? I don't want you to do anything.'

'Where's that son of yours?'

Charlotte's mouth went dry. 'Why?'

'No particular reason. I just wondered. Isn't he going to get bored while you're working?'

Charlotte pulled her hands out of her pockets to put them on her hips. 'And what would you suggest I do with him? Bring him here? He's not a baby. He can look after himself. Heavens, lots of children back home have to look after themselves all day while their parents go out to work!'

Logan held up a hand to halt her tirade. 'All right, all right,' he exclaimed. 'I only asked a perfectly innocent question. It occurred to me that—well, that he might find Carlos's company better than none at all.'

Charlotte stilled the tremor in her voice. 'He—he's quite used to entertaining himself. My—my husband didn't give a lot of time to him, so there's no need for you to concern yourself on his behalf.'

Logan shrugged. 'Surely he had friends in England,' he suggested quietly, and she sighed frustratedly.

'What does it matter to you?'

'I like him,' replied Logan flatly.

'Well, he doesn't like you!' retorted Charlotte childishly, and completely ignoring what she had said to Robert earlier added:

'So please—leave him alone!'

Logan's lips thinned. 'Very well. If you insist. But I think you're allowing prejudice to get in the way of common sense. However ...' He rubbed absently at the hair on his chest. 'We shall see.'

Charlotte turned her back on him, and went to knock more vigorously at the door, and this time, much to her relief, she heard definite sounds of activity inside. A few seconds later the screen door opened, and Lisette Fabergé appeared, scantily clad in a broderie cotton wrapper and little else. Her hair was untidy from the pillow, and a streak of the previous day's mascara ran down one cheek. She looked at Charlotte with disgruntled eyes, and then caught sight of Logan. Immediately her expression softened, and she even managed a smile.

'Have I overslept?' she exclaimed dramatically, and Charlotte knew that she was only pretending concern. 'Oh, heavens, and on your first day, too, Mrs Derby!'

'It's all right, really——' Charlotte was beginning, when Logan interrupted her.

'Is there anything you want from San Cristobal today, Lisette?' he asked. 'I have to go over to the harbour to see Dan Herbert, so if there's anything you need ...'

Lisette frowned consideringly, and then a howl from Isabelle brought an exclamation of impatience from her lips. Charlotte glanced briefly round at Logan, and then she said: 'I'll attend to her, shall I?' and brushed past the other girl before she could make any objection.

The smell of stale food in the bungalow was nauseating, but after the first grimace of distaste Charlotte pressed on. As she had guessed, Lisette's bungalow was identical to her own, and besides, Isabelle's noisy whereabouts were not difficult to locate.

The children's bedroom contained a single bed and the cot Isabelle was using. As Logan had surmised, there was no sign of Philippe, and a pair of pyjama trousers tossed carelessly on to the floor indicated that he had dressed before leaving. The room was filled with the acrid aroma of Isabelle's wet nappy, and the little girl was sitting miserably among a pile of tumbled bedding, chewing at her fist between yells.

Charlotte flung open the shutters, flooding the room with light and fresh air, and then she turned to the cot and

47

lifted the unhappy infant into her arms. 'It's all right,' she reassured her gently, as Isabelle cast a rather doubtful look at her rescuer, and then she grimaced again at the disordered room. Toys were strewn everywhere, and no attempt had been made to fold the clothes that were tossed about on bed and dressing table alike. Whatever qualities Lisette Fabergé possessed, tidiness did not appear to be one of them.

Isabelle was starting to whimper again, and guessing the baby was hungry, Charlotte decided to get her a biscuit at least before tackling anything else. But when she emerged into the hall again, with the baby in her arms, Logan had come up on to the verandah, and was leaning against the doorpost talking to Lisette. His eyes lifted to encompass her slim presence, and the years sped away and she was sixteen again and back in the garden of the nursery in Richmond, with Logan standing there waiting for her. As if his thoughts corresponded with hers, his relaxed indolence disappeared, and the coldness of his eyes was chilling. Then he straightened, bade Lisette a curt farewell and turned away, descending the verandah steps without a backward glance.

CHAPTER FOUR

'WELL!' Lisette allowed the screen door to slip from her fingers. 'That was sudden, wasn't it?'

Charlotte evaded a direct reply. 'Do you have any biscuits?' she asked, gesturing towards Isabelle. 'I—I think she's hungry.'

Lisette wrinkled her nose. 'I'm sure she is, but don't you think she needs changing first?'

'I'll change her. And give her a bath. But surely she can have a biscuit meanwhile.'

Lisette shrugged. 'There are some in the kitchen, I think. Make yourself at home. You might as well. That's what you're here for, isn't it?'

Ignoring the insolence in the other girl's voice, Charlotte carried the baby into the kitchen, staring, appalled, at the pile of dirty dishes in the sink. She looked round despairingly. Where would one find anything here? The remains of the previous evening's meal still reposed on the table, and the flies crawling over it made her feel positively sick.

Isabelle began to whimper, and balancing her on one hip, Charlotte began opening cupboard doors. She eventually found a half empty packet of digestive biscuits, and the baby took the proffered sweetmeal eagerly. There was a high chair pushed against one wall, and Charlotte pulled this out and put Isabelle into it while she cleared the table and scraped the decomposing food into the wastebin. By the time Lisette reappeared, again dressed in the grubby shirt and pants she had been wearing the day before, Charlotte had the dishes half done, and the kettle was boiling.

'Three cheers,' observed the other girl dryly, 'what a busy little bee you are.'

Charlotte finished drying the dishes. 'Not really,' she

replied. 'Do you want me to make you some tea—or coffee?'

Lisette drew a packet of cigarettes out of her trousers' pocket and put one between her lips. 'No,' she said at last, applying the flame of a match to her cigarette. 'I think I can just about manage that. You go ahead and deal with Isabelle. I'll appreciate the chance to smoke a cigarette without interruption.'

As Charlotte was sure Lisette smoked a good many cigarettes without interruption, she made no comment, but as she was carrying Isabelle through the door a thought struck her.

'Philippe?' she asked. 'What about him?'

'What about him?' demanded Lisette irritably.

'He's not had any breakfast, has he?'

Lisette lounged into a chair. 'Oh, I expect the Stevens' will feed him,' she remarked indifferently. 'If not, he'll come back when he's hungry.'

Charlotte stared at her. 'Aren't you worried about him?'

Lisette looked up at her, her blue eyes challenging. 'Why should I be? He can't get lost. Not here. And the people who live in Avocado Cay all know who he is. No one would harm him. They have too much respect for Logan.'

Charlotte would have turned away then, but now Lisette detained her. 'You knew Logan before you came here, didn't you, Mrs Derby?'

Not knowing how much Logan had told her, Charlotte nodded. 'Briefly.'

'Was that before or after your marriage?'

Charlotte's hesitation was only momentary. 'After,' she stated definitely. 'Some years after. If you'll excuse me ...'

Bathing Isabelle was both a pleasure and a release. The uncomplicated task of soaping the baby's chubby body, and sharing in the delight she gained from kicking her fat little legs, helped to erase the knowledge of her own duplicity, to justify the defensive lie she had just told.

It was for Robert's sake, she told herself fiercely, and refused to consider it further.

There were clean clothes in the drawers in the children's room, and she dressed Isabelle in a cotton top, with a scalloped edge, and matching panties that concealed the ugly disposable nappy. With her quiff of reddish hair combed into a curl on top of her head, she looked adorable, and it was all Charlotte could do to keep from cuddling her. It was so long since Robert had allowed such a show of emotion, and there was so much comfort to be gained from a child's embrace. But she controlled her feelings, realising as she did so how accustomed to doing so she had become.

Lisette was still sitting in the kitchen when she returned, but embarrassment or plain common decency made her assert herself when Charlotte reappeared, taking Isabelle from her and saying: 'I'll give her her breakfast, Mrs Derby. You make yourself a cup of coffee or something.'

'Not right now, thanks.' Charlotte had no desire for a cosy *tête-à-tête* with Lisette. 'I'll go and tidy up the children's bedroom, and sort out the dirty clothes for washing.'

'Well, you don't have to do the washing,' remarked Lisette laconically. 'Carlos does ours along with his and Logan's. He's quite a handy bloke to have around, as no doubt you'll find out.'

'Oh, but——' Charlotte opened her mouth to say that surely the baby's things should be washed separately, and then closed it again. It wasn't her business, after all.

Lisette seemed to guess what she had been about to say, however, and gave her a wry look. 'I'm no liberationist, Mrs Derby, but I see no reason to work myself to a shadow when Carlos can just throw them all into his automatic, okay?'

'Of course.' Charlotte lifted her shoulders in assent, and went back along the hall to Philippe and Isabelle's room.

She began to see later that morning why Lisette was so lethargic. In spite of the sea breeze the bungalow became

51

very warm, and she was sweating freely by the time she had cleared up all the toys and made the beds. On impulse, she had entered Lisette's bedroom and found it to be in just as much of a state as the children's, and although she wasn't being paid for housework, she felt obliged to make the bed and fold the discarded clothes.

It was twelve o'clock before she knew it, and all hopes of going down to the beach to see Robert had been banished. However, when Philippe arrived back, grubby but unharmed, from the Stevens', and Lisette began opening tins of soup for their lunch, Charlotte suggested that she might go down to her own bungalow to see her son.

'Of course. Go ahead,' said Lisette indifferently, spooning Isabelle's baby dinner into another saucepan. 'You needn't hurry back. We all take a rest in the afternoons. If you come back around four, that should be time enough.'

Charlotte made no objection, although she couldn't see that it was good for a woman of Lisette's age to spend so much time in bed. Still, that was not her concern, and she hurried down the slope to her own bungalow with a lightening heart.

The place was deserted, however, and there was no sign of Robert. Trying not to give in to the panic that threatened to engulf her, she sluiced cold water over her face and neck, and set off to look for him. He had to be somewhere about, she told herself firmly. Philippe had been absent all morning without Lisette turning a hair. Robert was seven years older, and therefore that much safer.

All the same, this was a new environment for him, she thought uneasily, remembering their argument that morning about swimming out of his depth. Accidents could so easily happen, and there might be currents in the lagoon that he didn't know about.

The beach stretched away to a wooded headland in one direction, and towards Logan's beach house in the other. *Logan*, she thought, with a mixture of relief and apprehension. That was where she would find him.

She tramped determinedly along the sand, kicking off her sandals to make walking easier. In other circumstances, she would have enjoyed the feeling of the fine coral sliding between her toes, but right now she was in no mood to enjoy anything. She was hot, and tired, and entirely out of countenance with herself.

As she approached Logan's beach house, she began to drag her feet. What if Robert wasn't there? What if they hadn't seen him? But they must have done, she told herself impatiently, before the absence of the station wagon reminded her that Logan had intended going over to the other side of the island that morning. But there was still Carlos. In fact, her feet quickened again, Carlos was a much easier proposition than Logan.

There were chairs set on the verandah of the beach house, and the steps which led down to the beach were set at the side of the building. Louvred doors stood wide revealing ranch-style timbering, and an assortment of junk littered the floor. Oxygen tanks and rubber aspirators stood cheek by jowl with photographic equipment, huge spotlights indicating work done after dark. There was snorkelling equipment, too, and face masks, looking like the accoutrements of some latterday monster.

But right now Charlotte wasn't much interested in the tools of Logan's trade. With every passing minute her anxiety for Robert was growing, and Carlos's sudden appearance at the top of the steps brought a shocked gasp from her lips.

'Oh!' she said, putting the palm of one hand over her mouth. 'You startled me.'

'I'm sorry, ma'am.' Carlos was apologetic. 'Is there something I can do for you?'

Charlotte's heart sank. 'You mean—you don't know why I'm here?' she protested weakly.

Carlos frowned. 'No, ma'am.'

'Robert's not here, then?'

'That would be—your son?'

'Of course. Of course, my son. Have you seen him?'

Carlos came down the steps towards her. 'Not lately, ma'am.'

'You saw him earlier on?'

'Well, he was on the beach this morning. I saw him just after Mr Logan left for San Cristobal.'

'Just *after*?' Charlotte swallowed convulsively. 'You're sure it wasn't before?'

'No, ma'am.' He paused. 'Mr Logan wouldn't take him off somewhere without your permission.'

Charlotte sighed. Was she so transparent? 'Then where is he?' she cried desperately, turning to survey the whole beach.

And then she saw him, trudging nonchalantly towards them from the direction of the headland, something which looked suspiciously like her sponge bag dangling bulkily from his fingers.

'Isn't that your son coming now?' Carlos pointed, as his eyes simultaneously picked up the small figure foreshortened by distance, and Charlotte had to agree.

'Yes. Yes, that's him,' she said ruefully. 'I—well, I'm sorry I troubled you.'

'No trouble, ma'am.' Carlos's dark eyes were amused. 'But he looks to me like a young man who can take care of himself.'

'Oh, he can.' Charlotte sighed. 'Better than I can, I sometimes think.' She began to move away. 'Thank you, anyway.'

'Any time,' Carlos nodded, and went back up the steps.

Charlotte crossed the sand to meet Robert with scarcely concealed irritation. Because of him she had had to go to Logan's house and humble herself before his servant, knowing full well that when Logan returned it was the first thing he would hear. In addition to which he might misconstrue her motives, particularly as it appeared that Robert had been doing nothing more dangerous than shell collecting.

In consequence, her tone was sharp as she demanded: 'Where have you been? And what have you got there?'

Robert, his bare shoulders already showing signs of tanning, stared at her in surprise. 'What does it look like I've been doing?' he countered cheekily, and she clenched her fists.

'It might interest you to know that I've been half out of my mind with worry!' she snapped, turning back to the house, and heard his sigh of resignation.

'Oh, Mum!'

'Don't "Oh, Mum" me! And who gave you permission to take my toilet bag?'

'It was the only thing I could find.'

'For what?'

He held up the bulky bag. 'Rock samples.'

'Rock samples?' Charlotte's echo of his words was exasperated. 'Why do you want rock samples?'

Robert gave her an outraged look. 'They're fascinating! Those limestone cliffs over there ...' he gestured towards the headland, 'they're very old. I might have some fossils among these, and volcanic rocks. If the islands are as old as Mr Kennedy says, there should be heaps of mineral samples. Who knows, those cliffs might once have been the ocean floor, before some great eruption thrust them away.'

'Where did you get all this?' inquired Charlotte suspiciously.

'From books.' Robert was indignant. 'I'm not making it up.'

'I never thought you were.'

'I think I'd like to be a geologist when I grow up. Our physics master, Mr Turner, used to say that man's whole evolution could be traced through studying the earth's crust.'

Charlotte reached the shade of the bungalow with relief and climbed the steps. 'Well, the next time you intend going on a geological expedition, do you mind leaving me a note?' she tossed at him over her shoulder, and Robert dug his fist coaxingly into the small of her back.

They had a simple lunch of scrambled eggs, and then while Robert examined his rock samples, Charlotte put her feet up on the couch in the living room.

'Did you go swimming?' she called, wriggling her toes, and Robert looked back at her from the verandah.

'Some,' he admitted briefly. 'Did you have a good morning? What's Madame Fabergé like?'

'Madame Fabergé is English, did I tell you?' She lifted her eyebrows interrogatively, and he shook his head. 'Well, she is. And I don't think she's very happy here.'

'Why not?' Robert frowned.

Charlotte sighed. 'I don't know. I think she probably misses the trappings of civilisation. And of course, with her husband dying like that, and leaving her with two young children ...'

'Yes.' Robert was thoughtful. 'I heard Mr Kennedy say her husband was dead.' He paused. 'Is he going to marry her, do you think?'

'Who?' asked Charlotte evasively, playing for time.

'Mr Kennedy.' Robert stared at her impatiently. 'I mean, why else is she here?'

Charlotte pretended to adjust the cushions behind her. 'I believe neither she nor her husband have any family, and as—as Mr Kennedy was her husband's best friend ...'

'... he's taking care of her,' finished Robert consideringly. 'Well, perhaps he is.'

Charlotte chose to ignore the suggestion behind her son's words, and closed her eyes. There was still a couple of hours before she was due back at the Fabergés'. Time enough to relax for a while, if she could ...

She must have slept because the sound of voices awakened her to the fact that they were no longer alone. She sat up jerkily, vaguely disorientated, to find Philippe squatting beside Robert on the verandah, discussing the merits of his finds with him. The sudden transition to consciousness was unnerving, however, and she got up unsteadily from the couch to make herself a cup of tea.

But it was almost four, and she gulped the tea too hotly for enjoyment, and leaving Robert with instructions not to get into any mischief, made her way back to the Fabergé house. The sea beckoned as it had not done earlier in the day, and she thought how marvellous it would be to submerge her overheated body in its cooling depths. Maybe later, she promised herself with a sigh, and pushed open the bungalow door.

Lisette was sitting reading magazines on the verandah at the back of the house, from where it was possible to see Logan's beach house and the wooden landing where the ketch rocked on its mooring. A tray of tea beside her, plus an ashtray overflowing with stubs, indicated she had just had refreshment, but she didn't offer the other girl any tea.

'Where's Isabelle?' asked Charlotte, looking about her, and Lisette gestured carelessly over her shoulder.

'She woke up a little while ago, so I gave her a biscuit and a drink of orange juice, and now I suppose she's playing,' she replied in a bored voice. 'You can go and bring her out if you like. Oh, and there's a pram in the living room, you know, if you feel energetic.'

Loath to make criticisms, nevertheless Charlotte couldn't resist asking: 'Do you take her for walks?' and Lisette's lips thinned.

'No, I don't,' she retorted brittlely. 'I'm not the type to enjoy cosy domesticity. I married Pierre to escape from all that. What a mistake that was!'

The temptation was to linger and ask her exactly what she meant, but Charlotte decided she had heard enough. She was not here to listen to Lisette's complaints, particularly when she did not honestly get the impression that the young widow mourned her husband's death. Perhaps she blamed him, for leaving her unprovided for, although she was lucky in having Logan to care for her. Charlotte's resentment flickered. Lucky indeed ...

Isabelle was standing on her wobbly little legs, happily throwing the contents of the cot on to the floor. The sheets and pillowslip had been separated and lay scattered round the bedroom, while the remains of the biscuit her mother

57

had given her had been squeezed into a gooey mess all over the bars of the cot.

Charlotte retained her patience with difficulty. The room which only that morning she had restored to order looked almost as messy now as it had done before she began, and Lisette was to blame. If she had lifted Isabelle after her sleep instead of leaving her to her own devices all would have been well. As it was, Charlotte felt obliged to tidy up again.

Isabelle began to protest at her continued confinement and closing the door, Charlotte lifted her out of the cot and set her on the floor while she remade the cot, replacing the rubber sheet and spreading a clean sheet over it. With new frontiers to explore, the little girl crawled about happily, getting under Charlotte's feet but otherwise causing little trouble. It was obviously a new departure for her, and Charlotte wondered at the selfishness of a mother who could disregard her children's needs so entirely. No wonder Logan had decided to hire a nursemaid. If only it had not been her!

She collected a damp cloth from the kitchen and was endeavouring to clean the bars of the cot when she heard the sound of a car's engine. Guessing it was the station wagon, she continued with what she was doing, hoping Logan would be gone before she emerged. She could hear their voices, Lisette's, raised an octave higher, as it always was with him, and Logan's huskier baritone. She was probably offering him tea, thought Charlotte wryly, lifting a box of tissues out of Isabelle's grasp, and she jumped almost guiltily when the bedroom door opened to admit Logan's lean figure. Grim eyes surveyed the scene in one sweeping glance, and she wondered uneasily what it was she had done wrong now. Isabelle created a brief diversion by crawling rapidly towards the open doorway, but Logan anticipated her action and closed the door behind him, leaning back against it.

'What are you doing in here?' he demanded without expression, and she knew he was not addressing the child.

'I'm just tidying up,' she replied, annoyed to hear the note of conciliation in her voice. Then, more aggressively: 'Why?'

'You were not employed as housekeeper,' stated Logan, evenly, but she could tell he was restraining a harsher tone. 'You've only just arrived on the island, and my instructions were that you should take things easily for the first few days.'

'*Your* instructions?' Charlotte's temper was rising.

'I am your employer,' he reminded her coldly. 'You would do well to remember that.'

'And what am I supposed to do when I find that Isabelle has stripped the cot and smeared chewed-up biscuit all over it?' she inquired pleasantly.

'That is Lisette's—Madame Fabergé's—affair. Your only task is to take care of the children.'

'Really?' Charlotte jeered at his lack of perception. 'And you think I should have gone out to—to Madame Fabergé just now and asked her to come and clear up the mess in here?'

'Yes.'

'Oh——' She could think of no suitable retort. 'Do you think she would have come?'

'That has nothing to do with it.'

'On the contrary,' exclaimed Charlotte angrily, 'that has everything to do with it! Your—your—Madame Fabergé would probably tell me to go to hell, and with every justification. In my experience, *servants* do not tell their mistresses what to do.'

'You're not a servant!' snapped Logan, equally angrily. 'All right, perhaps you shouldn't suggest Lisette clears up the room, but if you left it, she would have to.'

'Would she?' Charlotte turned away as Isabelle bumped her head on the corner of a chair and started to cry. Picking the child up, she added: 'If I don't mind what I do, why should you?'

For several seconds, her gaze locked with his, brown eyes faltering before blazing amber. Then with a stifled oath, he wrenched open the door again and left her.

When Charlotte eventually deemed it safe to emerge, Lisette was alone. She looked round maliciously as the other girl appeared however, and said accusingly: 'Nobody asked you to clear up after Isabelle, you know.'

Charlotte gasped. 'I know that.'

'So why did you go complaining to Logan? For God's sake, leave the bungalow alone. It will be just as bad to-morrow whatever you do today.'

A thought for the week, thought Charlotte dryly, but she didn't say it. 'Look, I don't know what—what Mr Kennedy has been saying to you, *madame*,' she was beginning, when the other girl interrupted her.

'Call me Lisette, for heaven's sake! she exclaimed. 'I never did go much for that Madame Fabergé bit. It's not me. And I'm pretty sure you don't call Logan Mr Kennedy when you're alone either.'

Charlotte couldn't prevent the wave of colour from sweeping revealingly up her face. 'I haven't been complaining,' she insisted, and Lisette shrugged her shoulders indifferently.

'All right, I'll take your word for it.' But her eyes narrowed speculatively. 'Come and sit down. It's time we got to know one another. Both being widows, we ought to have something in common.'

Charlotte shied away from the implications behind this gesture. 'As a matter of fact, I was thinking I might take Isabelle to paddle,' she suggested uncomfortably, and saw the way Lisette's lips drooped.

'Oh, very well,' she muttered, reaching for another cigarette. 'Go and play nanny. But don't imagine I don't know there's something fishy going on, because I do!'

Robert and Philippe were in the water, and Charlotte hoped anxiously that her son was not overdoing it. Too much sun was worse than too little, and although it was cooler now, to his vulnerable skin it was still quite hot. To her surprise, the younger boy could swim like a fish, and

Robert waded into the shallows to explain that Logan had taught him.

'Mr Kennedy's also told him that when he's older, he'll teach him snorkelling,' he added with evident envy. 'I wish he'd teach me.'

Charlotte bent to Isabelle to hide her expression. 'I thought you didn't like him,' she murmured, as Robert kicked frustratedly at the creaming ripples. 'My, isn't the water warm!'

Robert hunched his shoulders. 'I wish you'd tell me what you and Mr Kennedy were rowing about,' he muttered.

Charlotte straightened to look at him. 'Why? So you could justify making friends with him?' she challenged, and then felt a pang at Robert's pained expression.

'No. No,' he protested, in a muffled voice. 'Only——'

'Robert, what you decide to do about Mr Kennedy is your own affair!'

'Is it?' He looked at her uncertainly.

Charlotte sighed, feeling mean and petty, but she couldn't help what she was about to say. She was tired. It had been a long day, and Robert's words were the culmination of all her fears.

'Look,' she said tensely, 'if you want to be friends with the man who in the past has hurt and humiliated me, then go ahead! I shan't stop you! If learning to snorkel and skin dive means more to you than supporting your mother, then don't let my feelings stop you!'

'Oh, Mum!' Robert's cry revealed the basic insecurity behind his confident façade and Charlotte was immediately ashamed of her outburst. But the words could not be withdrawn, and she could see from his expression that she had hurt him deeply by suggesting he might betray her.

Shaking her head, she lifted Isabelle into her arms, and turned back towards the bungalows. 'I'm tired, Robert,' she said, by way of an explanation. 'Don't stay in the water much longer. And take a shower when you get back to the house.'

Philippe decided to walk back home with her, and once his initial shyness had been breached, he chattered on quite happily about what he had done that day.

'You haven't swallowed anything you shouldn't, have you?' Charlotte asked, forcing a lightness she was far from feeling, and the little boy giggled.

'No,' he said, shaking his head definitely. 'Uncle Logan said if the safety-pin had been open, I'd have had to eat cotton wool sandwiches to stop it from hurting my tummy. Ugh! I wouldn't have liked that.'

'No, I imagine not,' agreed Charlotte dryly, wishing she had Philippe's facility for reducing everything to basics.

By the time she returned to her own bungalow, shadows were deepening over the sand dunes, and a velvety dusk scented the air with a musky sweetness. She could hear the sound of crickets in the rough grass that grew between the palm trees, and from the village drifted the evocative rhythm of a small combo. It could be on record, she guessed, or more likely there was a bar where one could go and take a cool beer.

Robert was in the living room when she went in, the swim trunks he had been wearing earlier in the day exchanged for the inevitable jeans and a tee shirt. He was flicking through the pages of a comic he had brought with him from England, and barely glanced up when she arrived.

'Gosh, I'm exhausted!' she remarked, as an opener, and he shrugged his thin shoulders.

'I'm not hungry if you don't feel like making dinner,' he said.

Charlotte sighed. 'Well, I am.' She pushed her shoulders back, curving her spine. 'What do you fancy? I know there's some steak. I saw it at lunchtime.'

'Steak is fine,' responded Robert indifferently, and controlling her impatience, Charlotte went through to her bedroom.

The sea shore beckoned, but she turned away from its temptation and took a shower instead, making the water

62

icy cool to sharpen her senses. Then she dressed in lemon silk pants and a printed wrap-around smock that was cool as well as comfortable.

In her absence, Carlos had provided an assortment of foods for their dinner. There was the steak she had seen earlier, as well as salad and fruit, and a dish of dressed crabmeat. Robert came to support himself against the door jamb as she was boiling some sweet potatoes to add to the salad she was preparing, and she said lightly: 'There's crab as well as steak. Which do you prefer?'

Robert shrugged. 'Which do you?'

'Steak, I think. We had cold chicken and salad yesterday.'

'Fine.'

'You want that, too?'

'Whichever is easiest.'

Charlotte's patience stretched. 'If you don't care what you eat, why don't you go away and leave it to me?'

A flush of colour darkened his cheeks. 'I haven't seen you all day,' he muttered, once more awakening the guilt inside her.

'I have to work, Robert,' she protested, spooning oil and vinegar into a basin. 'We've both got to adjust to our new— circumstances.'

Robert hunched his back. 'And do you like it here?'

'Do you?'

He pulled a face. 'It's all right.'

Charlotte sighed. 'What happened to your fossils?'

'You mean the rock samples,' he corrected her. 'They're in my room.'

'Have you classified them?'

'What does that mean?'

Charlotte gave him an old-fashioned look. 'You know— sorted them out? Made a list of what they are?'

Robert shook his head. 'I haven't got any books to look them up in. I was going to——'

He broke off abruptly and she frowned. 'What were you going to do?'

'Oh, nothing.'

'Come on!' She felt exasperated. 'Finish the sentence.'

'Well, I—I thought I might—might ask...'

He was silent for so long that she finished it for him. 'You thought you might discuss them with Mr Kennedy, didn't you?' Robert still said nothing, so she added: 'So what's stopping you?'

He looked woodenly at her, and she bent to her task again. 'Robert, you're making this very difficult for me... Just because I don't want you discussing our private affairs with Mr Kennedy...'

'I wouldn't do that!' he protested.

'So—if you want to be a friend of his, I can't prevent you.'

'Not much,' he muttered, and she lifted her head.

'What did you say?'

He turned away. 'Call me when it's ready, will you? I'm going to unpack the rest of my things.'

Charlotte expelled her breath noisily, and then resumed what she was doing with unnecessary vehemence. She had to be practical about this, she told herself fiercely, uttering an angry imprecation as the egg she had been about to break slipped out of her hand and smashed on the floor. Alienating Robert's affections was the last thing she ought to be doing at this time, and the more she tried to keep him and Logan apart, the more desirable the relationship would become, in Robert's eyes at least. Why didn't she just opt out of the contest, let Robert make friends with whom he liked, and then wait for the inevitable cooling that would come with familiarity?

She dropped the paper towels that she had used to mop up the broken egg into the waste bin. If only it was that simple! But it wasn't. Robert was a great talker. Who knew what conclusions Logan might draw from the boy's conversation, particularly if he happened to reveal that Matthew Derby had not been his father? Her greatest fear was that Logan might discover the truth, and in so doing destroy once and for all the love she and Robert shared. What would Robert do if he ever discovered Logan was his father? What would he think of her for keeping the truth from him, particularly now?

Her head was aching by the time she set the meal on the kitchen table, and while Robert appeared to enjoy his, she pushed her steak round the plate and only picked at the potatoes and salad. If this was Logan's idea of tormenting her, he could have no idea how successful his scheme had been. Why he might have done it bore further consideration, but right now she only wanted to lay her head on the pillow and forget.

CHAPTER FIVE

CHARLOTTE stood at her bedroom window, looking out on the sweep of deserted shoreline, palely illuminated by the light of the moon filtering between low-hanging clouds. It had been raining earlier in the evening, and Robert had gone to bed in disgust, muttering about the weather on San Cristobal being no better than England on occasions. But she had known he was bored, and the rain had only been an excuse.

She sighed. If it seemed much longer than eight days since they had come to Avocado Cay to her, what must it seem to the boy, cut off from all but the most immature company, that of Lisette's son Philippe? It was true he enjoyed swimming and sunbathing and exploring the outcrops of the headland, but it was natural that a child of his intelligence should need more than a four-year-old's conversation to exercise his brain. She did her best to talk to him in the evening, but often she was tired herself, and more inclined to relax with a book than talk about the island's ecology.

During the day they had progressed as far as the village, but the children they had seen there were much younger than Robert, and he had nothing in common with them. His upbringing had been such that he was just as at home with adults as children, and consequently his isolation was more acute.

Since their initial disagreement over his association with Logan, nothing more had been said, and as far as Charlotte knew he kept firmly away from that end of the beach. She guessed it must be frustrating for him when Philippe treated Logan's house like his own, and came and went without invitation, but he had not mentioned it again. To Charlotte, however, his avoidance of the subject was in some ways worse than an open confrontation might have been.

The sea moved lazily along the rim of the beach, and a strange restlessness filled her. She had retired to bed some time ago, but after tossing and turning for over an hour she was no nearer achieving the oblivion she sought. Perhaps a walk along the beach might relax her more satisfactorily than lying here allowing the tortuous writhings of her thoughts to torment her.

She looked down at her cotton gown, which was one of Matthew's nightshirts adapted for her own use. She could hardly go out in that, but it was easy to step into the silk culottes she had worn that evening, and she didn't need anything else.

Barefooted, she let herself out of the house, stepping down on to the still warm sands with a curious feeling of release. The fine coral was unexpectedly rough against her skin, the soles of her feet acquiring a sensitivity that gave her the sensation of feeling every grain.

The sea beckoned with its age-old mystery, but she had more sense than to swim alone, and at night. She had been in the water a few times during the past week, but always with Robert and Philippe in attendance, and usually when she could be sure that Logan was not about. He and Carlos seemed to take the ketch out a lot, and from Philippe's childish chatter she had established that they were diving off the reef. She guessed it had something to do with Logan's purpose here on the island, but the situation with Robert being what it was, she never asked questions.

Now she walked towards the ocean, arms crossing her breasts, hands gripping her shoulders at either side. The rain earlier had left a coolness in the air that nevertheless had a velvety feel to it, and the wind tugging at her hair was pleasant after its confinement of the day. She breathed deeply, closing her eyes for a moment, inhaling the scent of the sea. There was something elemental about the night, she thought, feeling the tenseness inside her easing away, some spiritual presence that made one supremely aware of one's own insignificance. Beside the unceasing ritual of the elements, what minute place did man hold in the scheme of things?

Charlotte opened her eyes again to a strange prickling at the back of her neck, and the awareness of eyes upon her of which she had no conception, and then gulped as a dark shadow rose from the waves a few yards in front of her, and came walking out of the water towards her.

She froze to the spot, unable to turn and run as instinct dictated, and then felt weakness envelop her as she recognised Logan's lean figure. But even as this fact registered, so, too, did another, and her cheeks flamed as her eyes took in his unashamed nakedness.

She turned abruptly away, and then halted when he said: 'Charlotte!' in a low impatient tone.

'Yes?' She didn't turn, but she heard him approach her, and as he came round to face her, she saw with relief that he had hitched a towel about his hips.

'Surely the sight of a man's unclothed body is no novelty to you!' he exclaimed tersely, and she hugged herself more closely.

'There are bodies—and bodies,' she retorted.

Logan said a word she neither understood nor wanted to. 'And what was *his* body like, hmm?' he demanded savagely. 'A man of almost sixty. Was it soft—like *I* know yours is? Thick and smooth and sinuous ... Or gnarled and pouched, like an old prune!'

'I don't have to listen to this,' she got out chokingly. 'If you'll excuse me——'

'Charlotte!' His voice was rough with emotion. 'Please! All right, I'm sorry. I shouldn't have said that. Don't go in, not yet.'

'I don't see that we have anything to say to one another,' she managed unsteadily. 'For some reason best known to yourself, you allowed me to come here, but I don't have to talk to you. Particularly not at this time of night. I only came out for some air——'

'Oh, *Charlotte!*' He raked back his wet hair with a

frustrated hand. 'Don't you see? This is the only time we can talk!'

'No, I don't see that.'

'But you came out here.'

'Not knowing I would see you, believe me!'

His features tautened at the insult. 'You don't pull your punches, do you?'

'Why should I?'

'For God's sake, Charlotte, I've been very patient.'

'Patient?' She stared at him. 'You? What are you talking about?'

He fixed his eyes on some point above her head as if looking at her disturbed his thought processes. 'Tell me about your husband,' he commanded thickly. 'Tell me about Matthew Derby. I want to know all about him. I want to understand how your feelings towards him changed so dramatically. So dramatically in fact that you bore his child in the first year of your marriage! What did you think about the first time he made love to you? Tell me that. Make me see it, Charlotte.' His fists clenched by his sides. 'Paint me a picture. Destroy, once and for all, this hunger I have to repeat *our* experience!'

'Logan!'

His eyes lowered to hers. 'What's the matter? Have I shocked you? You shouldn't be so sensitive—not now. We both know what happens when a man wants a woman, don't we? It's an insatiable thing that eats into his flesh, until he's blinded by his own emotions. God, Charlotte, you can't have completely forgotten what it was like with us! Unless Matthew was so much better at it than I was, and I won't accept that.'

Charlotte knew then she had to get away from him. His words were too insidious, invoking as they did images she did not want to remember. He had no conception of how easy it was for her to recall that brief taste of happiness, but the bitter aftermath hardened her heart.

'You're so arrogant, aren't you?' she flung at him. 'What's the matter, Logan? Does it offend your manhood to suggest that I might have enjoyed myself more with someone else? Is that what all this is about? Do you want reassurance that your efforts were not inadequate?'

It was a foul thing to suggest, and as soon as the words were spoken, Charlotte was contrite. Logan was staring at her as if he couldn't believe what he had just heard, and her hands went involuntarily out to him, her fingertips encountering the cool dampness of his arms.

'Oh, Logan!' she cried, and suddenly he was close to her, and his mouth was covering her parted lips.

She had forgotten what it felt like to be kissed as Logan was kissing her. For eleven years she had been afraid to invite Matthew's kisses, knowing as she did how revolted she had felt at the touch of his wet mouth. Those kisses he had bestowed on her had been gentle pecks on her cheek or her forehead, casual salutations acceptable as such. Anything more would have been unthinkable, and therefore even Logan's mouth was an assault on her senses. But fear and revulsion quickly gave way to a mounting sweetness, and when he released her lips for the few moments it took to draw her down on to the sand beside him, she felt a fleeting anguish.

His skin was smooth, more roughly textured than hers, but sleek and flexible beneath her palms, his warmth and maleness enveloping her and making her overwhelmingly aware that only the thin material of the culotte suit separated them. He held her face between his hands, and his hardening mouth was echoed throughout the length and breadth of his body. She felt herself yielding weakly beneath him, and his hand slid from her shoulder, across her throat to find the zipper at the front of her suit, impelling it steadily downward.

'No, Logan,' she breathed, but he pulled the hands with which she might have resisted him around him, arching her body so that he could observe her reaction to the thrusting aggression of his with sensual satisfaction.

'No?' he probed with gentle mockery, his mouth seeking the pointed fullness of her breasts now exposed to his gaze.

'Why not? It's what we both want, don't deny it.'

'Logan, please . . .' she moaned, twisting beneath him, but her movements only dislodged the loosely-hitched towel, so that with an impatient exclamation he tossed it carelessly aside.

'You're so beautiful,' he muttered hoarsely, moving against her. 'When I think of you and that—that swine Derby——'

'Oh, don't, Logan, don't,' she pleaded, but when his mouth found hers again, she could not restrain the ardour of her own response.

'God, I want you, Charlotte,' he spoke against her lips, his warm breath filling her mouth. 'But you can feel that, can't you? A man never can hide his feelings.' He broke off roughly. 'God, I was a fool to think I could bring you here without—— I can't keep away from you!'

'No, Logan!'

'What do you mean—no? You want me——'

'*No, Logan!*'

Somehow Charlotte struggled up from the depth of a sexually-induced lethargy. It wasn't easy, when her whole body threatened to betray her, but his words were too similar to the words he had used to her once before, and she remembered only too well what had happened next. Lying here on the sand, seduced by the night, with Logan's weight imprisoning hers, the musky scent of his body filling her with the desire to surrender to the primitive needs he aroused inside her, it would be fatally easy to succumb again to the dark fascination he had for her. But she couldn't. She mustn't. Not because she didn't want to, but because he must never suspect the power he had over her, not only for her sake, for Robert's, too.

At first, Logan resisted her efforts to get away from him, but when she cried: '*Let me go!*' in a tearful tone, he smothered a groan and rolled on to his back, setting her free.

She sat up quickly, her fingers fumbling with the zipper, conscious all the while of Logan lying beside her, and of the potent attraction of his lean body. God, she thought unsteadily, what am I doing here? And then, more wildly: Why am I leaving him? *I want him!* But not on his terms, the still small voice of sanity reminded her, and she struggled to her feet.

Logan opened his eyes then and looked up at her, the moonlight glinting on his strained features. 'We are not through, Charlotte,' he told her flatly, reaching for the towel and standing up. 'But run away, if you must.'

'We are—we are through,' she blurted tremulously. 'At least, so far as I'm concerned——'

'No.' He shook his head, draping the towel around him. 'I sometimes think we haven't even begun.'

'You said ...' She hesitated as his words came back to her. 'You said you—*brought* me here?'

'That's right.' His lips twisted as he turned to stare broodingly out towards the veiled horizon. Then he looked back at her again, and she winced at the grimness of his expression. 'You didn't imagine finding me here was co-incidental, did you?'

'But——'

'It's too late to go into explanations now,' he said expressionlessly. 'Besides, I don't know that you deserve them.' He stretched his shoulders. 'Goodnight, Charlotte. We have plenty of time to talk, don't we? Sleep well!' And with this parting taunt he strode away along the beach towards his own house.

Charlotte watched until his shadow was absorbed by the deepening shadows cast by the lowering clouds. As if to remind her of the uncertainty of the weather, a few drops of rain drifted to her on the breeze, and the wind made eerie moaning sounds between the trees about the dunes. Realising she could not stand here all night, she clenched her fists and turned back to the bungalow, running the few yards to the verandah as if to rid herself of the daunting apathy into which she was sinking.

She went inside, closed the door, and was turning the key in the lock when Robert said, almost laconically: 'Does

72

that mean I can be friendly with Mr Kennedy now, Mum?' and she almost jumped out of her skin.

Pressing a hand to her throat, she sought to distinguish his whereabouts in the darkened interior, and then blinked dazedly when he flooded the room with electric light. 'Wh-what are you doing up at this hour?'

Robert didn't answer her, gesturing instead towards her pale, shocked features. 'Hey, did I startle you? I'm sorry.'

'Sorry?' Charlotte's teeth jarred against each other. She straightened away from the door, checking that the zipper was in place. 'Robert, you could have given me a heart attack, frightening me like that!'

'Well, I've said I'm sorry.' Robert spread his hands, young, and disruptively like the man she had just left in his sincerity. 'What more can I say?'

She turned on him irritably, ready to make some abrasive retort, and then changed her mind as other thoughts struck her. 'How—how do you know where I've been? Have you been spying on me?'

Robert looked injured. 'No!'

'Then how do you account——'

'I got up for a drink,' he told her through tight lips. 'Your bedroom door was open, and I—I was worried about you. Then—then I saw you—both.'

Charlotte pushed back her hair with a nervous hand. 'I see.'

'I won't tell anyone what I saw, if that's what's worrying you!' he muttered, in an undertone, and all the love she had for him spilled over in one devastating surge.

'Oh, Robert, Robert!' she whispered tremulously, and the next minute his hard young arms were around her, and he was hugging her tight.

'I'm sorry, Mum,' he mumbled. 'I didn't mean to spy on you, honestly. I just looked out, and then—and then—I couldn't look away.'

'It's all right, love, it's all right,' she reassured him urgently, not at all sure that it was. A wave of perspiration drenched her body when she considered what had so nearly happened, but how much had he seen? How much had he understood?

'You're not angry with me, are you?'

'No. No, of course I'm not angry with you ...'

'And—and is it all right if I make friends with Mr Kennedy now?'

Charlotte felt hysterical laughter welling up in her throat and swallowed it back with difficulty. Oh, Robert, Robert, she thought wonderingly, what would I do without you to keep me sane?

Lisette was in an ugly mood the next morning. She was already up and dressed when Charlotte arrived at the bungalow, a far from usual circumstance for her, and she started in on the other girl immediately, complaining that Isabelle's dungarees were not where she had left them, and that since Charlotte came to *help* her, she had not been able to find anything!

The injustice of this made Charlotte want to retaliate in kind, and tell Lisette that far from confusing the issue she had in fact created order from chaos. She would have liked to have added that until she came she doubted whether Lisette had known Isabelle possessed any dungarees, considering she had unearthed them from the bottom of Philippe's toy cupboard. But she bit back what would have undoubtedly developed into a slanging match, and collected the little girl's trousers from the drawer where they were folded and politely handed them over.

Lisette snatched them from her hand without gratitude, rolling the protesting Isabelle over her knees, and hauling them on over her nappy without ceremony. Then, looking up and seeing that Charlotte was still standing there, she raised her eyebrows interrogatively.

'Well?' she demanded. 'What are you waiting for? I'm perfectly capable of giving Isabelle her breakfast. Go and make the beds like you usually do.'

Charlotte hesitated, prepared to challenge that order,

but then shrugged her shoulders. After all, she had encouraged Lisette to treat her as housekeeper. She could hardly object now if the situation didn't suit her.

'Uncle Logan's gone away,' remarked Philippe, from his position on the floor with his toy cars. For once he had not disappeared before breakfast, and this in itself should have warned her that all was not as normal. Even so, she was disturbed by the feeling of dismay that filled her at this news. It no doubt also accounted for Lisette's behaviour, too.

'Has he?' she asked, but Lisette prevented him from enlarging upon the subject by exclaiming impatiently: 'For goodness' sake, get those cars out of here, Philippe! If you can't play in your own room, then you'd better take them outside.'

Philippe shrugged his shoulders philosophically, and got to his feet, gathering the handful of cars into his arms. But he dropped one and then another, and Charlotte bending to help him seemed to infuriate Lisette still further.

'Leave him alone!' she snapped, and Isabelle, recognising the tone of her voice and thinking it was for her, started to scream. 'Oh for heaven's sake!' Lisette suddenly changed her mind and thrust the baby into Charlotte's arms. 'You deal with them. I've got a headache. I'm going to my room.' And she marched out, snatching up her cigarettes on the way.

Left to themselves, Charlotte and Philippe exchanged glances. 'Mummy wanted to go with Uncle Logan,' the little boy explained candidly, and although she knew she ought not to listen to him, Charlotte couldn't help herself. Besides, there was something else she wanted to know.

Putting Isabelle into her high chair and silencing her objections with a rusk, she said casually: 'Does—does your uncle go away often?'

Philippe had subsided on to the floor again, cars and all. 'I don't know,' he answered with the inconsequence of any toddler. 'Look—do you like my Mercedes?' He made a screeching noise with his mouth. 'That's what Uncle

Logan says it is—a Mercedes. He said he used to have a Mercedes.'

Charlotte forced a tight smile. 'Lucky Uncle Logan!'

Philippe looked up. 'Can I have custard for breakfast?' he asked, startling her by his lightning change of conversation.

'Custard?' she echoed, without enthusiasm.

'Yes.' Philippe looked at her appealingly. 'When Daddy was alive we used to have custard for breakfast. He liked it, too, you see.'

Charlotte regarded him sceptically. The idea of a Frenchman who liked custard for breakfast was not convincing, and she had learned enough about Philippe in the past week to know that he could be as devious as anyone else. Somehow he had learned that by mentioning his father's name he could depend on a favourable reaction to almost any request he cared to make, but Charlotte, having had experience with the sometimes calculated emotions of children, guessed he seldom if ever thought of his father these days. Maybe when he was older he would regret what had happened, but right now Philippe lived in the present.

'If you like custard so much I'll make some for you at lunchtime,' she promised, disregarding his despondent expression. Then: 'I wonder where—Uncle Logan has gone?'

'If I tell you, will you make me some custard?' demanded Philippe eagerly, and her colour deepened in embarrassment.

'No, I won't,' she retorted, determining never again to give in to the impulse to question a child. 'Now, come and have your cereal like a good boy.'

Robert had laid the table and put the kettle on to boil when she returned home at lunchtime. It was a pleasure to see his cheerful face after the morning she had spent. The Fabergé children had somehow taken their mood from their mother, and had both been as difficult as they could be, so that Charlotte felt utterly exhausted.

It was wonderful just to sink down into a chair and kick off her shoes and relax.

Carlos must have been down, because there were fresh rolls still wrapped in the napkin, and her eyes widened in amazement when Robert produced a dish of deliciously smelling curry from its warming place under the grill.

He allowed her to stare at him disbelievingly for a few minutes, and then he grinned. 'No,' he said, shaking his head, 'I didn't make it. Carlos did. It was supposed to be for him and Mr Kennedy, but he said it would just be wasted now.'

Charlotte brought her back away from the chair. 'Mr Kennedy's gone away,' she said, achieving what she hoped was a casual tone, but Robert already knew.

'He's gone to St Thomas,' he said, answering her unspoken question. 'His boss is staying in *Charlotte Amalie*.' His eyes twinkled. 'Did you know about that? *Charlotte Amalie*, I mean.'

She shook her head. 'I may have heard it somewhere. But how do you know all this?'

'Well ...' Robert hunched his shoulders, 'I took you at your word, and went along to the pier. I was looking at the boat when Carlos came out. Do you know what? The boat has an engine as well as sails, and he says he'll take me out in it tomorrow. Isn't that terrific?'

'Terrific!' echoed Charlotte without enthusiasm. 'Robert, I hope you haven't been making a nuisance of yourself. I'm sure—Carlos must have things to do——'

'Oh, Mum!' Robert stared at her indignantly. 'Of course I didn't make a nuisance of myself. I think—well, I think Carlos was quite glad of my company. Some people are, you know.'

'Now don't start that again.' Charlotte had had enough of fractious children for one day. 'About the curry ...'

'Yes?'

'Whose idea was that?'

He flushed. 'Well—mine in a way,' he muttered honestly.

'Robert!'

'Well! Carlos was going to throw it out, and I told him you were sometimes tired when you got back from the Fabergés', so he said I could take it, if I wanted to.'

Charlotte heaved a sigh. 'I see.'

'It was no use to him, Mum, really.'

'Wasn't it?' She was more doubtful. Then she sighed: 'Look, what is Carlos having for his lunch today?'

'How should I know?'

'Well, I suggest you run along to the beach house and find out, and if he'd like to come and share this curry with us, tell him—he's very welcome.'

'Oh, boy, yes. Yes!' That apparently met with his approval. 'I won't be long,' and he darted out of the room on eager feet.

As soon as he had gone, Charlotte regretted the impulse which had made her suggest such a thing. What was she doing encouraging him to mix with Logan's assistant? Just because last night he had cornered her into a reluctant admission of her own involvement with Logan it did not mean she could not retract it in the morning. And yet how could she without alienating him once more? Not for the first time, she contemplated the difficulties coming here had created for her. But Robert was a boy who enjoyed masculine pursuits, and although she didn't doubt his love for her, forcing him to choose between pleasing her and himself might cause irreparable damage. And Logan was nobody's fool. He had only to see Robert in a certain way . . .

She got up from the chair, her hands clenched, all thought of relaxation forgotten. And she had been dismayed that Logan had gone away, she thought bitterly. She ought to have been cheering. The longer he stayed away, the sooner her month would be up, and she could return to the real task of finding a home for herself and her son.

CHAPTER SIX

IN fact, much to Robert's evident disappointment, Carlos turned down their invitation to lunch.

'He said he'd already had a sandwich,' Robert explained dejectedly on his return. 'But I don't think he wanted to come.'

Charlotte sighed. 'Why not?'

Robert shrugged, lounging into a chair at the table. 'I don't know. I just got that impression.'

'Well ... If that's so, what of it?' Charlotte tried to make light of it. 'Come on! Have some curry, or it's going to be wasted.'

Robert propped his elbows on the table, supporting his chin on his knuckles. 'Perhaps you were right,' he muttered. 'Perhaps I was in the way.'

Charlotte sank down into her own seat wearily. 'Don't be silly, Robert. Eat your curry, and stop looking as if you'd lost a pound and found a penny.' Conversely now she found herself adding: 'He wouldn't have offered to take you out to the reef tomorrow if he hadn't wanted your company.'

Robert looked up, doubtful at first and then gaining in confidence. 'Hey, that's right,' he exclaimed. 'I'd forgotten about that.'

'There you are, then.' Charlotte tried to keep the irritation out of her tones. 'Now, can we talk about something else, please?'

But in the days that followed, she found it impossible not to play some part in Robert's enthusiastic discussions of his day's activities. She learned that Logan was making a scientific exploration of the reef for the Mendoza Institute of Oceanography in Rio de Janeiro, that he was studying the coral, and cataloguing the varying species of underwater life that made their homes in and around its living skeleton. Robert came home full of stories of things he had seen from the deck of the sailboat, and once he brought her a large conch shell which he explained Carlos had found on the ocean floor.

'It's a queen conch,' he told her proudly. 'Carlos says that probably something—like the larva of a marine worm, for instance—got inside the shell, and because there wasn't enough room, the conch died. Isn't that sad? A huge snail like that dying because of a worm!'

'Men have died for less,' remarked Charlotte dryly, twisting the conically shaped shell between her fingers. 'I've seen these things in handicraft shops back home. They're quite expensive. Are you sure Carlos said you could keep it?'

Robert nodded. 'Yes. He said you might like to have it for an ornament. He's got others. He says the meat from them is really tasty, too.'

Charlotte put down the shell. 'Not for me, thank you.'

'Oh, Mum!' Robert laughed at her. 'You could easily have eaten it without knowing what it was. Carlos says that if you pound it first, it tastes just like veal.'

'Really?' Charlotte was beginning to get tired of what Carlos had said. 'Robert, don't you think it's time you were getting ready for bed? It's almost half past nine.'

Logan came back towards the end of the week.

Charlotte had not known when he was expected, and had almost succeeded in convincing herself that those moments on the beach had been his idea of amusing himself at her expense. She had decided that he would be as glad as she was when her four weeks were up.

But then Robert came home one lunchtime with the news that Carlos had had word that Logan was arriving back that afternoon, and that he was bringing his boss with him, and all her anxieties were revived.

'That's Manoel Mendoza, of course,' Robert went on

knowledgeably. 'He owns the institute in Rio that pays for Mr Kennedy's expeditions.'

Charlotte sighed, her brief period of tranquillity shattered. 'I suppose Carlos told you that, too.'

Robert regarded her half defensively. 'Yes. Why not?'

'It just seems to me that Carlos tells you rather a lot,' Charlotte replied equably. 'What do you tell him?'

Robert coloured. 'What do you mean?'

'I mean if you have these conversations, you must make some contribution to them.'

The boy shrugged and turned away. 'I haven't told him much.'

Charlotte's fingers sought the rough edge of the kitchen table. 'Have you told him about—about your—that Matthew Derby was not your father?'

'No.' Robert shook his head. 'I told you I wouldn't talk about that. It's—personal.'

'Yes. Yes, it is.' Relief made her feel weak.

'Besides ...' Robert shifted his weight from one foot to the other, 'we don't even talk about it, do we?'

Charlotte caught her breath. 'We—we haven't,' she admitted, dreading what was to follow.

Robert hunched his shoulders. 'At—at first, I didn't believe *him*, you know,' he said, and Charlotte was shocked by her own ignorance of this possibility. 'I didn't,' he repeated, seeing her reaction. 'I thought it was just another way for him to try and hurt me.' He paused. 'But when —when he died ...' He shook his head. 'If I had been his son, we wouldn't be here, would we?' he finished logically.

Charlotte didn't know what to say, how to answer him. It explained so much, of course, but it left so much more to explain, and right now she did not have the courage to begin some inventive tale about his real father.

'When—when you realised Matthew had been telling the truth,' she ventured, 'how—how did you feel?'

'Towards you, you mean?' Robert shrugged his thin shoulders. 'I don't know. It's difficult to remember. It was all wrapped up with—with *him* dying, and Aunt Elizabeth

81

—well, Elizabeth anyway, saying that *he* had come to his senses at last and you didn't deserve any better ... I—I just wished I'd been older, that's all. I wished I'd been able to look after you, instead of you having to look after me.'

'Oh, Robert!' Charlotte felt the tightening in her throat. 'What would I do without you?'

Robert looked self-conscious. 'Well, anyway, all I told Carlos was that we used to live in Richmond and that I went to a private school. He seemed to know about—about you being a widow.'

'Yes. Yes, I expect he does.' Charlotte turned to the stove and lifted the pan of rice that was steadily boiling dry. They were back to basics again without Robert asking that impossible question. Contrarily, she wished he had. Not that she could have been honest, she thought bitterly, but it would have been out of the way. Now she said: 'Sit down. I've creamed the remains of the chicken we had last night, so I hope you like it.'

Halfway through the meal, however, Robert put down his fork and looked at her. 'You're not—well, sorry that Mr Kennedy's coming back, are you?'

Charlotte concentrated on her plate. 'Why on earth should you think that?' she exclaimed, guilt putting the irritation in her voice.

'Well ...' Robert was searching for words, 'that row you had with him when we first came here——'

'That's over, Robert.'

'I know it is. But—well, did it have something to do with me?'

Charlotte's cheeks flamed. 'With you?'

'Yes.' Robert's jaw jutted defensively. 'If—if Mr Kennedy was a friend of—of *his*, he probably knows I'm a bastard!'

Charlotte was on her feet almost before he had finished speaking. 'He doesn't know any such thing!' she cried. 'And don't ever let me hear you use that word again! You are not a—a——' She caught her lower lip between her teeth, biting hard. 'Robert, you were born after Matthew and I were married. To all intents and purposes, you are our son.'

'But I'm not, am I?'

Charlotte sank down into her chair again, aware that she was trembling. 'Robert, eat your lunch,' she begged.

He picked up his fork again, but his enthusiasm had gone. '*He* said my—my father was a student.'

'He was.' That at least was true.

'Why didn't you marry him?'

Charlotte drew an unsteady breath, realising that for all his brave talk, Robert was still very much a child. 'It was all a long time ago,' she said inadequately.

'Did you know who he was?'

She gasped, remembering Matthew's accusations. 'Of course I knew.'

'Then——'

Closing her eyes, she strove for an acceptable reason. Only one came to her: 'He—he was already married,' she told him reluctantly, opening her eyes apprehensively, half afraid of his censure.

But Robert seemed almost relieved. 'Was that all?' he exclaimed.

'All?' she echoed faintly.

'Yes. Some of the boys at school—their mothers had boy-friends. Harvo Pearson said he had so many courtesy uncles, his family tree must read like a monkey puzzle.'

Charlotte didn't know whether to feel shocked or relieved. That boys should discuss these things among themselves was an indication of the way things had changed since she was a child, but their understanding was both precocious and disquieting.

'I don't think I want to talk about it any more,' she said now, pushing her scarcely-touched meal aside. 'When—when you're older, perhaps——'

'That's all right, Mum,' said Robert airily, tackling his meal once more with renewed appetite. 'You don't have to say anything else.' He smiled at her. 'Gosh, this is good! It reminds me of that chicken suprême we used to have back—back in England. You're a jolly good cook, considering ...'

Now Charlotte wanted him to continue. 'Considering what?'

'Well ...' Robert moved his shoulders awkwardly. 'I mean, you weren't used to cooking and looking after things when you came here, were you?'

Charlotte frowned. 'I used to help Mrs Parrish, Robert. And I helped run the play group when you were just a toddler.'

'Yes, but you had it pretty easy, didn't you?'

Charlotte felt uneasy. 'Is that what you think?'

'Well ...' Robert looked discomfited now.

'Robert!'

'Oh, it was just something Carlos said.'

'Carlos?'

'Yes. He said you weren't used to hard work.'

'Oh, did he?' Charlotte's spine prickled with resentment. 'And what else has Carlos said about me?'

'Nothing, Mum. Honestly.'

'Are you sure?'

'Of course I'm sure.' Robert pushed back his hair with that familiar gesture. 'Er—can I have some more chicken, please?'

After Robert had gone for a swim later that afternoon, Charlotte was still brooding over what she had learned. Was Robert telling her the truth, or had Carlos said more than her son had admitted? And what kind of an opinion did Logan's assistant have of her anyway? How much did he really know about that early relationship? How long would it be before he alerted Robert to the knowledge that his mother had known his employer some time before her marriage to Matthew Derby? The trouble was, Robert knew too much, and she had Matthew to thank for that. But at least she and Robert had talked, and perhaps that would ease the situation.

She returned to the Fabergés' towards teatime as she

usually did, and was giving Isabelle her tea on the verandah when she heard Logan's deep voice inside the bungalow. She had not seen the car earlier, so he must just have got back, and her nerves tightened painfully at the awareness of his proximity. Lisette had apparently spent the whole afternoon preparing herself for his return, and Charlotte thought the other girl had never looked more attractive. In a becoming shirt-styled cotton, her curly hair washed and shining, she had greeted Charlotte with unusual amicability, apparently delighted that Logan was coming back.

But trying not to listen to their exchange now, Charlotte couldn't help but be aware of the resentment in Lisette's tones, and she wondered if she had been mistaken in assuming the other girl's attentions had been for him. Lisette's voice was rising, and quite clearly she heard her angry words: 'You can't expect me to agree, Logan! I will not have that man living in this house! If you must invite more guests than you can cater for, then you'll have to make other arrangements!'

'Lisette!'

Logan sounded impatient, but she was adamant, and a moment later Charlotte heard her bedroom door slam.

The silence which followed was unnerving. It was all Charlotte could do, to go on feeding Isabelle as if nothing untoward had occurred, to prevent herself from speculating on who Logan had brought back with him, and who he had asked Lisette to accommodate.

The screen door squeaked, and she glanced round apprehensively, instantly aware of her disadvantageous position, kneeling on the boards of the verandah by Isabelle's chair. Logan emerged to stand looking down at her moodily, his dark features ominously compressed. He was more formally dressed than she had seen him, in a beige silk suit and a bronze shirt, the matching tie pulled a couple of inches down from his loosened collar.

Isabelle gurgled and held out a hand to him, but for once he seemed immune to the appeal of the child. 'Good afternoon, Mrs Derby,' he greeted Charlotte politely. 'I trust you are well.'

Isabelle's dish was almost empty, so leaving her to scrape up the last shreds of fruit with her spoon, Charlotte got to her feet. It was the first time she had seen him since that night on the beach, but the space between had helped to restore her composure, and she could answer him equally calmly: 'I'm very well, thank you,' even if she did avoid looking directly into his eyes.

'Good.' He spoke almost absently, as if he wasn't really listening to her. Then: 'You heard my argument with Lisette, I suppose.'

'I could hardly help——'

'I am not criticising you, Charlotte,' he snapped, and she was taken aback by the harshness of his tone. 'It would have been impossible not to hear such——' He broke off abruptly. 'You'll know then that I have brought guests with me?'

Charlotte bit her lip. 'Carlos told Robert——' Then she, too, broke off as Logan's eyes narrowed speculatively.

'Carlos told Robert what?' he prompted. 'Since when are Robert and Carlos on such friendly terms?'

Charlotte was embarrassed now, and angry too, at the way he could so easily upset her. Taking a deep breath, she went on rather desperately: 'Carlos has very kindly spent some time with Robert while you've been away, and when he heard you were coming back, he said you might be bringing a—a Senhor Mendoza with you.'

'I see.' Logan inclined his head. 'But that was not quite what I asked. However, we will leave that for the moment. My immediate concern is to find accommodation for Carlos.'

'Accommodation for Carlos?' Charlotte echoed his words uncertainly. 'Oh—so that Senhor Mendoza can have his bedroom?'

'No.' Logan spoke evenly. 'So that Senhorita Mendoza can have his bedroom.'

Charlotte's mouth went dry. 'Senhorita ...?' She rescued

86

Isabelle's dish in an effort to divert Logan's attention. *Senhorita Mendoza,* she said to herself in confusion. Who was Senhorita Mendoza?

'Yes, Senhorita Mendoza,' repeated Logan patiently. 'Manoel's daughter, Elaine.'

'His daughter?' Charlotte realised she was making a mess of this. 'I'm sorry.' She straightened, the dish in her hand much to Isabelle's vociferous annoyance. 'Carlos didn't— that is, I didn't realise you were expecting two guests.'

'It was a sudden decision,' stated Logan flatly. 'Elaine wanted to come with her father. She's never been to Avocado Cay before, and this was the ideal opportunity.'

'With her father?'

'Yes.'

'And you can't accommodate her?'

'On the contrary, I can't accommodate Carlos.'

'I see.'

'Charlotte, Manoel can share my room, and Elaine will be very comfortable in Carlos's bed. Naturally, I can't ask her to sleep elsewhere.'

'Naturally.'

Logan gave her a narrow look. 'Are you being sarcastic?'

Isabelle's protests were becoming intrusive, and bending, Charlotte lifted the little girl into her arms. Then she looked at Logan again. 'No,' she answered him steadily. 'Of course not.' But she was—or at the least cynical, and he knew it. But who was this Elaine Mendoza? What was she to Logan? Another woman in his life? Why would she come to Avocado Cay unless . . .

Her speculations went no further. It was no business of hers, and the sooner she stopped behaving as if it was, the easier it would be.

Logan seemed to come to a decision. In two strides he had crossed the verandah and was descending the steps to the beach. Across the dunes, she could see Carlos unloading cases from the station wagon and carrying them into the beach house. No doubt Logan thought he had neglected his guests long enough, and irritation made her offer what common decency would not.

'Tell Lisette I'll see her later,' he threw over his shoulder, but she called him back: 'Logan—wait!'

'Yes?' He halted halfway down the steps, wary eyes on a level with hers.

'Robert—I know Robert wouldn't mind if Carlos shared his room,' she said quickly. 'So as not to inconvenience your guests!'

A savage expression crossed his lean face. For a moment she thought he was going to refuse her offer, and then he tugged angrily at his tie, pulling it off in one violent gesture. 'Thank you,' he said, through tight lips. 'I'll tell him what you've said.'

Charlotte watched him stride away across the sand, taking off his jacket as he went and throwing it over one shoulder. If she could *only* remember the painful things, she thought despairingly, instead of torturing herself with the bittersweet memories of love . . .

Lisette appeared as soon as Logan had gone which made Charlotte suspicious that the other girl had been listening to their conversation. Her face was streaked with mascara, however, and it was obvious that she had been crying.

'Well,' she said, glaring at Charlotte. 'So now we know, don't we?'

'Know what?' Charlotte was bewildered.

'Who our friends are!' retorted Lisette, sniffing. 'I suppose you thought offering Carlos a bed was a clever device, didn't you?'

'I don't know what you mean.'

'Don't give me that.' Lisette fumbled for her cigarettes. 'Logan didn't ask you to interfere, did he? You offered.'

'Well, why not?' Charlotte stared at her helplessly. 'Where else could he go?'

'Here.'

'Here? But you——'

'You heard Logan say he was coming back later, didn't you? He knew I didn't really mean it. Only I was so mad about—about——' She lit the cigarette with trembling ineptitude, throwing the match to the floor as it burned her fingers. 'Well, anyway, you needn't get any ideas in that direction. Dear Elaine's got it all nicely tied up.'

Isabelle was getting heavy, and Charlotte had intended to take her for a walk before it was time for her bath. But much against her better judgment, Lisette's conversation was becoming infinitely more appealing.

'You—know Elaine Mendoza?' she ventured reluctantly.

'Yes.' Lisette drew deeply on her cigarette. 'I know Elaine Mendoza.'

'What—what is she like?'

Lisette's eyes narrowed. 'You'd like to know, wouldn't you?'

Charlotte went scarlet. 'I—well, I was interested ...'

'Oh, yes, I'm sure.' Lisette settled her ample curves into a lounger. 'Well, why not?' She looked up at her through a veil of smoke. 'Elaine is one of those luscious Portuguese women—all almond eyes and olive skin. And fortunately for her, her mother is dead, and her father lets her have anything she wants.'

'I see.' Charlotte wasn't sure she wanted to hear any more, but Lisette wasn't finished yet.

'I met her in Rio about a year ago. You can imagine what I looked like then—six months pregnant, and about two stones overweight! Pierre ...' Her voice faltered for the first time when she used her husband's name. 'Pierre was with me, of course, and Logan, too. Elaine was just back from two years at a European finishing school, and believe me, no one was more "finished" than she was. Even Pierre positively melted beneath those liquid Latin eyes.'

'You make her sound quite formidable,' Charlotte remarked, attempting a carelessness that didn't quite come off.

'She knows what she wants,' said Lisette dryly. 'And right now Senhorita Mendoza is planning to be Senhora Kennedy.'

Charlotte had guessed, of course. Why else would a young woman with Elaine Mendoza's advantages want to come to Avocado Cay? There was nothing here, no theatres or nightclubs, not even an hotel. And the pleasure of sea and sand could be enjoyed just as well in St Thomas.

'Does that upset you?' Lisette asked now, and Charlotte quickly composed her features.

'Why should it upset me?' she countered.

'I don't know.' Lisette frowned. 'I don't get the relationship between you and Logan, but it's there, I know it.'

'You're imagining things.'

'No, I'm not.' Lisette was very positive. 'Anyway, I just thought I'd let you know you're wasting your time.'

Charlotte turned away. 'I'm taking Isabelle for a walk. I'll collect Philippe from the Stevens', shall I?'

Lisette shrugged moodily. 'If you like.' Then she kicked off her sandals, saying maliciously: 'It doesn't work, you know. Ignoring the obvious. Don't think I haven't tried?'

Charlotte put Isabelle into the canvas pram, and after fastening the straps over her chubby shoulders, pushed her up the track towards the village. Was she so transparent? she thought anxiously. If Lisette could see how Logan's presence disturbed her, could he see it, too?

It was almost a relief to talk to the Stevens. Michael Stevens had left a lucrative practice in South London five years before, to come and live on San Cristobal. His wife, Helen, had borne their two children here, and they seemed happier with the simple life. Philippe spent nearly all his time with four-year-old Tony, and his three-year-old sister, Anna, and Charlotte envied them their free-and-easy way of living. Helen had been a teacher, and she had endless patience with children, which was just as well, Charlotte thought, for Philippe's sake.

When she was walking back to her own bungalow that evening Robert came running to meet her, his eyes wide with excitement.

'Hey,' he exclaimed. 'Is it right? Is Carlos coming to stay with us?'

Charlotte was hot and tired after another of Lisette's tantrums, brought on no doubt by her dissatisfaction with the arrangements at Logan's house. She was in no mood to share her son's enthusiasm for an unwanted guest, and besides, how did Robert know anything about it?

'I thought I asked you to keep out of the way this afternoon?' she exclaimed, recalling her parting instructions.

Robert looked indignant. 'I did.' He hunched his shoulders, falling into step beside her. 'Mr Kennedy came to see me.'

Charlotte's heart skipped a beat. 'Did he?'

'Yes.' Robert sniffed. 'You always think the worst of me, don't you?'

'Oh, no, no!' Charlotte shook her head. 'What did— Mr Kennedy say?'

'Don't you know?'

Charlotte gave him an old-fashioned look, and he made a rueful grimace. 'Well . . .' he sighed, 'he asked whether I would mind if Carlos put up a bed in my room. I said no, naturally. I mean, it'll be fun, won't it? Having someone else living in the bungalow. And Carlos knows all about snorkelling and scuba diving and——'

'I'm sure Carlos is a mine of information,' returned Charlotte dryly, 'but he's not coming to *stay* with us, Robert. Just to sleep here. Mr Kennedy has guests——'

'Yes, I know.' Robert grinned. 'Miss Mendoza! I've seen her. She came to find Mr Kennedy.' He raised his eyebrows expressively.

Charlotte ignored the gesture and went up the steps into the bungalow. It was pleasant to be in her own home again, even if it was a temporary thing at best. And soon not to be entirely hers either, she thought wearily.

Carlos arrived with a camp bed and a sleeping bag after darkness had deepened the barrier of trees that separated them from the village. He entered the bungalow almost diffidently when Robert opened the door, and Charlotte guessed he was not wholly happy with the arrangements either.

Robert showed him into his bedroom, and Charlotte

could hear them talking together. There was an easy cama-
raderie between them that evidenced their growing relationship, and she wished there was someone she could talk to so
easily.

When Carlos emerged again, it was to say goodnight,
and Charlotte looked at him uncertainly. 'Do you usually
keep such early hours?' she asked, and a look of embarrassment crossed his dark face.

'Mr Logan, he thought perhaps you went early to bed,
Mrs Derby,' he replied, and she sighed.

'Not at nine o'clock, Carlos.' She looked up at her son.
'Robert goes at this time, of course, but there's no need
for you to emulate him, unless you want to.'

Robert's expression mirrored his disappointment. 'But
Mum ...'

'Your mother is right, Robert.' To her surprise and relief
Carlos backed her up. 'A boy should get his sleep. How
else can he expect to be fit enough to learn all the things he
has to learn?'

Robert sighed, but now he had other things on his mind.
'Carlos says that tomorrow he and Mr Kennedy might take
me out to the reef. I'm going to learn how to use a snorkel,
Mum. Isn't that great?'

Charlotte turned anxious eyes in the black man's direction. 'But——'

'He will be quite safe, ma'am,' Carlos assured her
quietly. 'I have hesitated to attempt his tuition until Mr
Logan returned, but there is so much to learn and enjoy,
and he is a sensible boy.'

Robert beamed. Then he turned to his mother again. 'You
don't mind, do you, Mum? Say you don't. I'll do exactly
as I'm told, honestly. Say I have your permission.'

Charlotte wondered what would happen if she refused.
Between them, they had put her on the spot, and whether
it was deliberate or not, little by little Robert was being
weaned away from her.

'Perhaps Mr Kennedy will be too busy to bother about
you while his guests are here,' she said, earning her son's

indignant stare. 'Now, off you go to bed. I'll see you in the morning.'

After Robert had left them, she wondered whether she had been premature in inviting Carlos to join her. After all, they had had little to say to one another thus far, and the only topics they had in common, those of her son and Logan Kennedy, she would rather avoid.

But, to her relief, it didn't work out like that. Carlos was an interesting man, having travelled with Logan through many of the tropical countries of the world, and his knowledge of the sea and its environs turned out to be quite fascinating. He could relate legends of sea monsters and shipwrecks, as well as describing to her the very real excitement a man could feel when faced with one of his natural enemies of the deep.

'I suppose you mean sharks,' Charlotte observed, remembering Robert's comments about attacks in shallow waters, and Carlos looked thoughtful.

'Some people think the barracuda is more dangerous than the shark,' he said. 'It's certainly more vicious, and more prone to attack. Then from a diver's point of view there are the giant clams. If one of them traps an arm or a leg, you don't have much chance of getting out alive.' He shrugged. 'Of course, sharks are dangerous, but scientists have discovered that it's possible to study them without being attacked. And they are, without doubt, one of the natural inhabitants of a reef, and therefore interesting in our work.'

Charlotte didn't like the images his words created, and hastened on: 'You're studying the reef, aren't you?' she hesitated, not wanting to probe. 'I wonder why reefs are formed.'

'That is a question that has puzzled scientists for generations,' replied Carlos, with a frown. 'Charles Darwin produced the first theory, and although other theories have been expounded, his is the only one to stand the test.' He rubbed his nose with a reflective finger. 'Darwin asserted that reefs began to grow around islands, but that as the island sank, as all islands do eventually, the coral grew higher and when the island disappeared completely, formed an atoll.'

Charlotte stifled a yawn. 'And what is an atoll?'

'Nothing more than a lagoon, completely surrounded by a coral reef.' He smiled. 'I am boring you, and you are tired.'

'Oh, no, you're not.' Charlotte was quick to contradict him. 'It's fascinating.' She gave an apologetic little grimace. 'It's these early mornings. The sound of the sea wakes me, and I can't get back to sleep again.'

Carlos rose to his feet. 'Then I suggest we call it a day, don't you?' He paused. 'And I want to say how grateful I am to you for allowing me to sleep here. We did not expect Senhor Mendoza's daughter to accompany her father to Avocado Cay, but ...' he spread his hands, 'women are unpredictable, as no doubt you appreciate.'

Charlotte stood up also, linking her hands together. 'We don't mind, really,' she assured him. Then: 'Lisette—Madame Fabergé, that is—explained that—that Senhorita Mendoza is a—personal friend of Mr Kennedy.'

Carlos inclined his head. 'Did she? Well, yes, I suppose she is. They've known one another for a number of years, at least.'

'A number of years?' echoed Charlotte confusedly. 'Oh, but—I mean, I understood they had met only a year ago.'

She was treading into private and confidential territory now, and her cheeks burned at the look in his eyes. 'I expect Madame Fabergé was referring to Senhorita Mendoza's return from Europe,' he replied equably. 'But Mr Logan first met the *senhorita* when he joined the Mendoza Institute seven years previously.'

'Oh, I see.' Charlotte wished she hadn't asked. What if Carlos told Logan that she had been inquiring about his relationship with Elaine? The ignominy of his amused enlightenment was something she could do well without. 'Er—is there anything else you need?'

Carlos shook his head. 'I shall probably be gone before

you are up in the morning, ma'am. If so, I shall see you tomorrow evening about the same time.'

Charlotte forced a smile. 'Yes.'

He moved towards the door, and then paused, looking at her intently. 'I shall not be indiscreet, ma'am,' he said quietly, and for an awful moment she thought he was talking about her relationship with Logan. But his next words disabused her. 'It is natural that you should be curious about Senhorita Mendoza, ma'am. You having known Mr Logan yourself for some years. No doubt you'll get to meet her tomorrow. And I believe Mr Logan is thinking of giving a dinner party while she's here.'

Charlotte made a display of shaking out the cushions on the couch. 'I'm sure Madame Fabergé will enjoy that,' she said, and taking the hint, Carlos bade her goodnight.

But in her own room, Charlotte felt far from sleepy. Why was she allowing Elaine Mendoza to occupy so much of her thoughts? She was a fool. No doubt this was just another ploy on Logan's part to try and frustrate her. He had already admitted to bringing her here under false pretences. Was his involvement with Elaine Mendoza intended to be the final humiliation?

She tossed restlessly on her bed, wishing she could close her ears to the insidious sound of the surf, which was a consant reminder of Logan's nearness. She would have liked to have walked again, to have fought the tugging wind in her hair, and calmed herself with the freedom of the elements. But Logan might be out there on the beach, and more disquieting still, he might not be alone...

CHAPTER SEVEN

LOGAN arrived next morning just as Charlotte was rinsing the breakfast dishes. Robert was in his room, and for a moment she thought it was his step in the hall, until the tall dark figure appeared in the doorway.

'Don't you ever knock?' she demanded, the restless night she had spent sharpening her tone, and Logan supported himself against the jamb, his expression hardening slightly.

'As a matter of fact, I did knock,' he retorted smoothly. 'However, as there was some doubt that you might still be here, I decided to find out for myself.'

Charlotte dried her hands on a paper towel, and ran nervous fingers over the buttons of her smock. She had found it cooler to work in dresses, and the loose styles of the moment only hinted at the rounded outline of her body beneath. Her hair was tied back with a chiffon scarf, the chignon proving impracticable where Isabelle's investigative fingers were concerned. For all it was early in the morning, his presence had brought a rush of colour to her cheeks, and she was unaware that she looked more like Robert's sister than his mother.

'Well?' she said now. 'What do you want?'

Logan's lips thinned. 'That is hardly the way to treat an employer, is it?' he remarked.

'I'm sorry.' She held up her head. 'But I'm afraid I don't think of you as my employer.'

'No?'

'No.' Then, realising how her words could be misconstrued, she added quickly: 'I mean, I never see you, do I? Lisette—Madame Fabergé—she always seems more like my employer than you do.'

'I can change that,' he reminded her dryly, and she looked down at her hands.

'What is it you want of me?' She despised the note of entreaty in her voice. 'I have to leave in a few minutes.'

Logan straightened and entered the room, immediately making her aware of its limited proportions. 'As a matter of fact, I came to discuss your working conditions,' he said, inserting his thumbs in the low belt that circled his hips. 'It occurs to me that you can't have had any time off since you arrived.'

Charlotte moved her shoulders indifferently. 'I'm off every afternoon,' she replied, realising how the days had run together since she came here. She had not been conscious of doing a job so much as filling in time until she could get away again. 'You don't need to worry about it.'

'But I do.' Feet apart, he successfully blocked any avenue of escape, and for once she wished Robert would put in an appearance. 'By the way, Carlos tells me he has already discussed with you our idea of teaching your son how to use a snorkel.'

'He mentioned it, yes.'

'But you have doubts.'

'Did he say that?'

'No. But I can see it.' One hand left his belt to support himself against the table. 'Perhaps if you knew a little more about it, you would feel less anxious.'

Charlotte ran a nervous hand over her hair. 'I—if you think he's capable of it, who am I to protest?' she returned shortly. 'Now, if you'll excuse me——'

His hand came out to detain her, fastening round her upper arm with firm assurance. 'Charlotte,' he said roughly, and she was close enough to feel the heat emanating from his body, 'I want you to come out with us while Elaine is here.' He held on to her when she struggled to free herself. 'I mean it, Charlotte. Listen to me. I intend to speak to Lisette——'

'You can't govern what I do in my own time!' she protested. 'And besides, I don't want to come out with you.'

'I mean—in the ketch,' he emphasised, but still she shook her head.

'I've said I'll let Robert go with you,' she exclaimed. 'Don't involve me in your plans.'

'I want you to come with us, Charlotte,' he snapped. 'My God, what do I have to say to persuade you? Must I remind you that so long as you are living at Avocado Cay, I decide when and for whom you expend your energies!'

'That's—*feudal*!'

'It happens to be the way I do things.'

'Oh, yes!' She was scornful. 'I know how you do things, Mr Kennedy!'

'I doubt you do,' he retorted, through tight lips. 'But we'll let that go.'

'I came here to help Lisette,' insisted Charlotte angrily. 'Not to make up a four for snorkelling!'

He regarded her with dislike. 'What's the matter with you, Charlotte? What did I ever do to you to make you treat me this way? I realise you must be bitter about Derby, but——'

'You don't know anything about it,' she told him tautly. 'Now, will you please take your hands off me?'

Logan released her abruptly, turning aside and thrusting both hands into the pockets of his denim pants, his quickened breathing evidence of his barely suppressed frustration. It crossed her mind that she ought to have more care in what she said to him, or he might begin to suspect that she had other reasons for despising him than the obvious ones. So far as he was concerned, she had been an experience which he wanted to repeat, and if finding she had married Matthew annoyed him, so much the better. But she must not allow her feelings to run away with her. He thought she was upset because Matthew had left his money to his brother, but that was all. She refused to consider those moments on the beach ...

'I intend to speak to Lisette,' he said now, in a restrained tone. 'I will not accept your refusal, and if I have to resort to other methods to get your compliance, I'll do so.'

Charlotte stiffened. 'What other methods?'

'Carlos told me that Robert thinks I was a friend of his father. I could disabuse him.'

Charlotte stared at him aghast. 'You wouldn't!'

'Wouldn't I? Why not? What have I got to lose?'

Charlotte brushed a hand across her forehead. 'Logan, why are you doing this? You've got me here—I'm doing the job I'm being paid for. Why should I have to help entertain your friends?'

Logan stifled an oath. 'It's not a question of entertaining my friends,' he snapped. 'I want your company. It's as simple as that.'

'Why? Isn't one woman enough for you?'

'Mum!' Robert's voice reached them before he did, but Charlotte could hear him coming along the hall, and she was pale when she turned towards the door. What a moment for Robert to choose, she thought distractedly, aware that her last words to Logan still hung in the air between them like skeletons at the feast.

'Mum, where are my—oh! Hello, Mr Kennedy.'

Charlotte dared not look at Logan, and she must have been holding her breath, because when he responded: 'Hello, Robert!' she gulped in air like a drowning man. She guessed it cost him an effort to continue evenly: 'What have you lost?'

Robert, noticing nothing amiss, pushed back his hair with a careless hand. 'Just my sandals,' he explained easily, lifting one bare foot. 'Did you come looking for me?'

'Not exactly.' Charlotte felt Logan's gaze flicker over her. 'As a matter of fact, I came to invite your mother to join us.'

'You did!' Robert turned excitedly to her. 'That's a super idea. You haven't done any sailing, have you, Mum? And you haven't had much time off since you came here.'

'Those were my sentiments, too,' observed Logan, regaining control. 'However, your mother seems to be shy of meeting my other guests.'

Robert looked surprised. 'Does she?' He looked at her.

'Are you, Mum? You needn't be, you know. Senhor Mendoza isn't at all frightening, and his daughter is really dishy! She said I reminded her of someone, but she couldn't think who.'

Charlotte wondered how taut nerves could be stretched before they snapped. As if Logan's behaviour towards her wasn't enough, now she had the anxiety of knowing that an outsider was already glimpsing the likeness between Robert and his father.

Licking her dry lips, she said wearily: 'I've just been explaining to—to Mr Kennedy, Robert, that I came here to help Madame Fabergé.'

'Oh, come on, Mum.' Robert seemed unwilling to comprehend the simple message she was trying to convey. 'You can stand a day off, you know you can. You were just saying how tired you were feeling at breakfast.'

Charlotte could have shaken him until his teeth rattled, but she knew he wasn't really to blame. Logan was the real culprit, and she guessed he was beginning to enjoy her discomfort. Her head was aching with the tension she was feeling, and she wondered how she could ever have imagined that he was a gentle man.

'I told you, Robert—I didn't sleep very well last night,' she exclaimed, and realised too late what an admission that was.

'Why didn't you sleep very well last night?' Logan took up her words at once, and she wished she had the courage to tell him exactly what she thought of him.

'I don't know,' she said at last, aware of Robert's eyes upon them. 'Does there have to be a reason?'

Logan shrugged. 'There usually is. Perhaps you're not getting enough fresh air. I think I must prevail upon you to join us, Charlotte.' His eyes dared her to contradict him. 'Tomorrow, hmm? And I won't take no for an answer.'

Charlotte made a pretence of consulting her watch. 'I must go. Lisette is expecting me.'

Logan stood aside. 'Of course. Will you tell her I'll be along to see her later in the day?'

Charlotte made no answer, but brushed past him on her way to the door, and Robert caught her hand. 'You will come tomorrow, won't you, Mum? I mean——' He flashed a quick look at the man. 'You and Mr Kennedy are still friends, aren't you?'

Charlotte wondered if Logan understood the meaning behind the boy's words, if indeed Robert had confided in him the scene he had witnessed between them on the beach. To consider such a possibility was to court further torment, and she didn't know how much more she could stand.

'I—I'll try and come tomorrow,' she conceded in a low tone, avoiding the second question, and Robert looked at her anxiously. But he had no idea what he was asking of her, and nor indeed did Logan. She was caught in a cleft stick—a cliché, but an apt one.

Lisette was in little better temper than she had been the day before, although it transpired that Logan had brought Elaine across to see her the previous evening.

'Condescending bitch!' she muttered, lighting another of her endless supply of cigarettes. 'She only came over here so that she could see how the other half lives! Thank goodness the kids were in bed, and the place was passably tidy.'

Charlotte lifted Isabelle out of her chair. 'I expect— Logan thought you might like to meet her again,' she said reasonably. 'After all, you've said yourself, life is pretty quiet around here.'

'The word is dull!' Lisette sounded petulant. 'Life is dull! God, I wish I'd never got married!'

Charlotte sighed. 'And what would you have been doing if you hadn't?' she asked patiently.

Lisette shrugged. 'I suppose I'd still be working at the institute in London.'

Charlotte paused. 'What institute in London?'

'The marine institute—the one attached to the university. I used to work there. I was a secretary. That's how I met Pierre.'

'I see.' Charlotte felt a pang. No doubt that was how Logan had met Pierre, too. When he was studying in London. It brought the whole thing closer somehow, and she was glad she had arranged to take Isabelle out for a walk, and could escape dwelling on the comparisons between her life and Lisette's.

But the other girl seemed to sense her withdrawal, and seized on it. 'Was that how you met Logan?' she asked curiously. 'When he was working in London?'

Charlotte shook her head. 'I—I don't really know what he was doing,' she lied quickly. 'It—it was my husband he was associated with.'

'Really?' Lisette sounded sceptical, and Charlotte couldn't altogether blame her. She was far too sensitive where Logan was concerned, and Lisette had time enough to speculate on the inconsistencies of her story.

'How did you meet your husband?' she asked now, and Charlotte could not evade an answer.

'As a matter of fact, Matthew knew my mother,' she admitted, at last. 'When my parents both died, he—he looked after me.'

'Adopted you, you mean?' Clearly, Lisette was intrigued.

'No, no, nothing like that.' Charlotte caught her lower lip between her teeth. 'He just gave me a home, that's all.'

'And when you were old enough, he married you?'

'Something like that.'

'But ...' Lisette frowned, 'if he knew your parents, surely he must have been quite a bit older than you were.'

'Yes, he was.'

Lisette shook her head. 'How much older?'

'Does it matter?' Charlotte had had enough of her questions. 'Lots of girls marry older men.'

'Not usually straight out of the schoolroom, they don't,' asserted Lisette. 'Heavens, how old is that boy of yours? Eleven? Twelve? You must have been about sixteen! Didn't you have any boy-friends of your own age?'

'I'd really rather not talk about it,' said Charlotte obstinately, realising that if she was not careful, Lisette might fasten on to the real truth of the situation.

'Why not?' Lisette examined the glowing tip of her cigarette. 'I guess you knew which side your bread was buttered, didn't you?'

Charlotte ignored that remark. 'I'll be back in about an hour,' she said, carrying Isabelle to the door, and Lisette pursed her lips irritably.

'What's the matter?' she demanded. 'Can't you stand to talk about him? You don't strike me as being particularly heartbroken by his death.'

'It's not that . . .'

'Then what is it?' Lisette shrugged. 'Oh, I know he didn't leave you anything. Logan told me that before you got here.'

'Did he?' Charlotte felt angry.

'Yes.' She grimaced. 'He said he'd hired some widow whose husband had left her without funds. I thought it was a pretty rotten thing for anybody to do.'

'Yes. Well, it wasn't quite that simple . . .'

'No?' Lisette raised her eyebrows. 'Why? What was he like? Was he handsome? Did he have stacks of money? Was that why you married him?'

'No!' Suddenly Charlotte wanted to defend herself. 'I —it may surprise you to know that I was very—fond of Matthew,' she declared. 'He—he wasn't particularly handsome, that's true, although he did look rather distinguished. But—well, he was always very kind to me. I don't care about his money. His family are welcome to it. That wasn't why I married him.'

'*Wasn't it?*'

Unaware, she had pushed open the door to the verandah with her hip, and while she was still talking to Lisette, Logan had come up behind her, his hand reaching past her to take the weight of the self-closing hinge. His nearness was disconcerting, as too was the scent of sweat from his body, and she started violently, holding so tightly on to

Isabelle that the little girl began to protest loudly at being squeezed.

Lisette got up out of her chair and came to join them. 'Logan!' she exclaimed, more warmly when she saw he was alone. 'Come on in.'

'Thank you.'

He took another step forward, and Charlotte had perforce to retreat into the room again to avoid him walking into her.

'I was just leaving,' she said, resenting the power he had over her, when even his appearance could set her pulses racing. 'Come along, Isabelle.'

'I'd rather you stayed,' Logan remarked, quietly, and now it was Lisette's turn to look annoyed.

'Why?' she asked. 'Is something wrong?'

'No.' Logan shook his head, looking infuriatingly calm, and Charlotte, guessing why he was here, wished she had not allowed Lisette to detain her. 'Nothing's wrong. I just wanted to ask whether you'd have any objections if Charlotte took tomorrow off.'

Lisette looked taken aback. 'Took tomorrow off?' she echoed. 'You mean—the whole day?'

Logan's expression was wry. 'Yes, the whole day. It may have slipped your notice, but she hasn't had any time off since she started here.'

Lisette turned angrily to Charlotte. 'Have you been complaining?' she demanded.

'No, I haven't.' Charlotte was indignant. She turned angrily to Logan. 'This is not my idea!'

'No. It's mine,' he agreed evenly. He looked at Lisette. 'Well? What do you say?'

'What do I say?' Lisette's lips worked soundlessly for a minute. 'What can I say? You're the boss.'

Logan's jaw hardened. 'You'll agree that all employees deserve some free time?'

'Well, yes, I suppose so.' Lisette flushed.

'Good.' Logan turned to Charlotte again. 'It's agreed, then?'

Charlotte wished she could refuse, but she had more to lose than he realised. 'I—I suppose so.'

'What's agreed?' Lisette looked suspicious.

'I'm going to teach Charlotte the rudiments of underwater exploration,' he replied, much to their mutual surprise.

'I see.' Lisette was first to recover. She gave Charlotte a narrow look. 'You didn't mention this before.'

'I didn't know,' Charlotte protested. Then as an idea occurred to her, she added: 'Why? Would you like to go in my place?'

'Lisette doesn't swim,' put in Logan dryly. 'Do you, Lisette?'

Lisette sniffed. 'I can't, can I? I have this ear condition,' she explained, for Charlotte's benefit. 'Swimming aggravates it.'

'I'm sorry.' Charlotte forced a smile for Isabelle's benefit. 'Well...'

'You're leaving?' suggested Logan, with annoying accuracy. 'Don't let me detain you any longer.'

The screen door banged behind her, and she wished his head had been in it. He had an irritating knack of always putting her on the spot, and now to add to her difficulties, Lisette was angry with her.

She pushed Isabelle's pram up to the village, collecting an assortment of helpers on the way. Philippe and the Stevens' children always attached themselves to her on her walks, but she had no illusions that the iced lolly she bought them at the tiny stores was not the attraction. Avocado Cay was really not much more than a collection of houses and a tavern, without any of the tourist attractions to be found in the larger resorts. Maybe at San Cristobal it was possible to hire a boat or go water-skiing, but according to Carlos, there were no large hotels there either. As yet, the island was unspoiled, and no doubt that was why Logan had chosen it for his explorations.

Thinking about Logan brought the morning's events back into focus, and she wondered what life here would have been like without his presence. It would certainly have been more restful, she thought, but would she have stayed on even so after the initial month was up? If Lisette Fabergé had been the Frenchwoman she had envisaged, and her husband simply a marine biologist, and not the man who had fathered her child and abandoned her, would she have been content? If she was completely honest with herself, she doubted it. Robert might not have found Monsieur Fabergé as sympathetic as Carlos, or Logan either, for that matter, and she knew now that he needed masculine company for at least part of the time. From her own point of view, San Cristobal had represented an escape, but from this distance the problems she had faced in England seemed paltry somehow. But was that because of what she had found here? she wondered, remembering that the Derbys had the power to strip the legitimacy of Robert's birth away from her.

She saw Helen Stevens working in her garden, and stopped to speak to her. The Stevens' bungalow was large and sprawling, its geography governed by their needs. Already a bedroom had been added, and a surgery where Michael could attend to his ever-increasing panel of patients; and as Helen had confided that she was pregnant again, Charlotte guessed that before long another room would be needed.

Helen was working in the vegetable garden. With admirable determination, she was attempting to grow peas and beans and potatoes, and the tall canes almost hid her from sight. But she stood up when she saw Charlotte approaching with the children, and said eagerly: 'Have you time for a coffee? I could do with a break.'

Charlotte hesitated. The delay would mean she would be out longer than the hour she had estimated, but as she had both children with her, she decided to accept.

It was cool in the Stevens' kitchen, and she deposited Isabelle on the floor among a pile of building bricks which Anna and Tony had abandoned. The three older children were having orange juice and biscuits outside in the shade of the verandah and the sound of their voices drifting in through the open doorway was relaxing.

Helen made the coffee, and then seated herself opposite Charlotte at the pinewood table. 'This is very pleasant, isn't it?' she smiled. 'I just needed an excuse to sit down for a while.'

Charlotte lifted the thin cotton of her shirt away from her back. 'I don't know how you do it,' she confessed. 'I think if I was pregnant, I'd be spending my time taking it easy.'

Helen shook her head. 'No, you wouldn't. You're not the type. Lisette—yes. You—no!'

Charlotte looked down into her cup, not wanting to be drawn into a discussion about Lisette, but Helen was not to be diverted. 'I think it's a pity if a young woman like her can't look after her own home and children! Good heavens, she doesn't even have a man about the place making a mess of everything you do!'

'Is that what Michael does?' inquired Charlotte dryly, and Helen smiled again, more ruefully this time.

'Oh, no. He's very good really. But you know what I mean.'

'If Lisette didn't need anyone to help her, I wouldn't be here,' Charlotte pointed out.

'No,' Helen conceded thoughtfully, tugging at a strand of brown hair. Like Lisette, she wore her hair short, but whereas Lisette's was inclined to curl, Helen's hair was definitely straight. Charlotte guessed she had once been an elegant woman, but now she seldom bothered with her hair or her nails, and went around mostly in shirts and slacks that did nothing for her somewhat angular figure. 'But you won't stay here, will you?'

Helen's words, coming so soon on her own thoughts along the same lines, startled her, and she took a few moments before she replied: 'I don't think so.'

'I thought not.' Helen grimaced. 'What I can't understand is why you took the job in the first place.'

Charlotte raised her cup to her lips, hoping Helen would

put her heated cheeks down to the temperature of the coffee. 'I wanted a complete change,' she said.

'Well, you certainly got that,' remarked Helen dryly. 'So what's changed your mind? Lisette?'

'No.' Charlotte shook her head. 'I—I have Robert to consider.'

'You always did.'

'Yes, well, I suppose I didn't realise the—conditions would be so different from what he's used to.'

'Is he unhappy, is that what you're saying?'

'No, he's not unhappy...'

'I thought not. Philippe says he's always with Carlos. I think that young man's had his nose put out of joint since Robert took over.'

Charlotte sighed. 'Oh, dear!'

'Don't be silly. Philippe needed a set-down. Logan spoils them all—including Lisette.' Helen ran a finger round the rim of her cup. 'So—if Robert's not unhappy, what is wrong? You don't object to him spending so much time with Carlos, do you? You're not—prejudiced or anything?'

'Heavens, no!' That was the last thing Charlotte wanted anyone to think. 'I—it's just—well, the schooling,' she finished lamely.

'You mean the lack of it, don't you?'

'Y-e-s.'

Helen shrugged. 'Send him to Tortola. There's a perfectly good school there. He could board through the week and come home weekends. Or there's always the States. Some people send their children there to school, but perhaps that's too expensive.'

'It is,' said Charlotte firmly. 'In any case...'

'There's something else,' said Helen shrewdly. 'There always is. Is it Logan?'

'Logan?' Charlotte could not have been more shocked. 'I—why, what do you mean?'

Helen sighed. 'I don't know. It was just something Philippe said.'

'Wh-what did he say?' Charlotte had to know.

Helen looked thoughtful. 'Oh, it was nothing much. You know how children chatter on. He just said something about Logan going away and you wanting to know where he had gone. It made me wonder whether you found him attractive—Logan, I mean. But knowing his commitment to Lisette...' She raised her eyebrows. 'It's always puzzled me why Logan's never married. I know he likes children. Perhaps after a decent interval, he'll marry Lisette.'

Charlotte finished her coffee and got to her feet. 'I must be going,' she exclaimed, and then realising she was inviting further speculation by not answering Helen's suppositions, she added: 'Perhaps marriage would be an unnecessary encumbrance—to Logan. He seems to do very well without it.'

'You mean the Mendoza girl, I suppose,' Helen nodded. 'Have you met her?'

'Not yet.' Helen shook her head. 'But Mike was talking to them both last night, and he said Logan said something about having a dinner party while the Mendozas were here, so I expect I shall. Mike says she's very attractive.'

'Is she?' Charlotte feigned indifference. 'I really have to go, Helen. Thanks for the coffee.'

'My pleasure.' Helen accompanied her to the door, giving Isabelle a biscuit to compensate for her extraction from the bricks. 'See you later, then. At Logan's place, perhaps.'

Charlotte forced a smile. She could hardly tell Helen that if she had her way she would be attending no dinner parties. It smacked too strongly of sour grapes, and that was the last thing she wanted to imply.

Philippe wanted to walk back with her for once, but when they reached the bungalow Lisette's temper had not improved, and he quickly disappeared again.

'I thought you said you'd be back in an hour!' she began, as soon as Charlotte appeared. 'I suppose you've been gossiping with Helen Stevens. Were you telling her about your invitation to join Logan and his guests? I bet she just loved hearing that. She doesn't like me, as if you didn't

109

know. What did she say? *Poor* Lisette! She never fitted in here!'

'I didn't mention it,' Charlotte retorted hotly. 'It may come as a surprise to you to learn that there are other topics of conversation beside you and Logan Kennedy!'

Lisette sneered. 'Oh, I see. Elaine came under the hammer, did she? She——'

'As a matter of fact we talked about Robert!' declared Charlotte angrily, and not altogether truthfully. 'I didn't think you'd have any objections to my being a little longer than I anticipated when both children were with me.'

Lisette reached for her cigarettes. 'It doesn't matter,' she muttered moodily. 'My feelings never do.'

Charlotte sighed. 'What is it now, Lisette? What have I done? If you're still annoyed about my taking tomorrow off——'

'And if I am? What then? What can you do about it?'

Charlotte took a deep breath. 'I don't want to go, but he is my employer, Lisette.'

'Oh, yes, that's very convenient, isn't it?' Lisette paced restlessly across the verandah. 'It may interest you to know that I had a visitor myself this morning. After Logan had gone.'

'Yes?' Charlotte was wary.

'Yes.' Lisette held up her head. 'Manoel Mendoza.'

'Oh!' Charlotte was impressed. 'That was unexpected, wasn't it?'

'It was rather,' agreed Lisette smugly. Then: 'He suggested I might like to join them for lunch tomorrow.'

'I see.' Charlotte wondered at the sudden plunging of her heart. 'And?'

'I had to refuse him, didn't I?' Lisette scuffed her bare toes irritably. 'Someone has to look after Isabelle, don't they?'

Charlotte sighed. 'Lisette, if there was some way——'

'Oh, don't bother making excuses.' Lisette would not be placated. 'And next time you want a day off, don't go running to Logan first.'

Charlotte deposited Isabelle in her chair. 'Shall I feed her?' she inquired quietly, but Lisette refused her offer.

'If I can manage tomorrow, I can manage today,' she retorted. 'And I shouldn't make any plans about staying on here after your month is up, if I were you.'

Charlotte didn't argue. There was no point. Lisette was in no mood to be reasonable. But she wished Manoel Mendoza had been with Logan earlier. How much easier it might have been then.

CHAPTER EIGHT

CHARLOTTE dressed with care the next morning. Not because she cared what Logan thought about her appearance, she told herself fiercely, but to give her the confidence to face Elaine Mendoza. Her white cotton trousers were immaculately creased, and the tangerine-coloured midi blouse tied securely about her rib-cage, leaving a couple of inches of pale flesh exposed to the sun. She tied her hair back with a white chiffon scarf, and was checking the contents of her raffia bag when Robert came to find her.

He whistled when he saw how she was dressed. Then he made an awkward gesture. 'Hey, Mum, this isn't a grand affair, you know. Jeans and a shirt; or just a bathing suit, that would do.'

Charlotte had been prepared for this. 'I felt like wearing something smart, for a change,' she said. 'Don't I look all right?'

Robert prowled round her. 'Sure, Mum, you look great! But honestly . . .'

Charlotte interrupted him to ask whether the swimming shorts he had on were all he intended to wear. Robert agreed that they were, and she did not object. Already his torso had acquired an all-over tan, and perhaps because of his Latin ancestry, he had not suffered any burning. She felt an anxious pang when she realised how his darkening skin would increase his resemblance to Logan, but now was not the time to have those kind of worries.

Carlos appeared as they were preparing to leave. He had risen earlier and gone to prepare breakfast for Logan and his guests, but now, Charlotte thought, Logan must have sent him back to make sure she didn't back out at the last minute. He, too, raised dark eyebrows when he saw her, but unlike Robert, he said nothing.

Logan was crouched on his haunches on the verandah of the beach house, examining the valve of an oxygen cylinder, when they walked up the steps. Like Carlos, he was wearing the frayed denim shorts Charlotte had seen him in before, and his eyes widened first and then narrowed between thick lashes when he saw her. Immediately he straightened, giving Robert a friendly smile before greeting his mother.

'Good morning,' he said politely. 'Thank you for coming.'

Charlotte opened her mouth to make some cutting retort, when a girl came out of the beach house to join them. Small and dark, dressed in a cotton zipped jacket with a cowled neckline, and a pair of bikini briefs, Charlotte stared at her in surprise. Was this Elaine Mendoza—this skinny little creature, with a fashionably frizzed hairstyle that seemed too heavy for her slender neck? And then Elaine turned to look at her through luminous almond eyes, and she knew why both Robert and Lisette considered her so attractive. Her pale features were perfectly formed, the bone structure refined and elegant, but her eyes and the full-lipped definition of her mouth were purely sensual.

'Hello,' she said, her voice a shade higher than Charlotte would have expected. 'You must be Robbie's mother.'

Immediately Charlotte was relegated to the position of belonging to another generation. But she refused to let it worry her. 'Yes, I'm Charlotte Derby,' she said. 'And you're—Miss Mendoza?'

'Elaine!' The girl's accent was overlaid with a European inflection, due no doubt to the time she had spent there. 'It's very nice to meet you, Mrs Derby.'

The situation established, Elaine turned back to Logan who had been watching this interchange rather enigmatically, and said: 'There you are, *querido*. I've saved you the trouble of making introductions, no?'

Logan was non-committal. 'Where's your father?' he asked, and Elaine gestured towards the house. 'He's com-

113

ing.' She turned to Robert. 'It's nice to see you again, Robbie.'

That Robert was captivated was obvious from the fatuous expression he was wearing, and Charlotte suppressed the desire to tell him to pull himself together and stop looking so foolish.

As if sensing her feelings, Logan attracted the boy's attention, suggesting that he might like to try out the diving equipment with Carlos while they waited for Elaine's father to join them.

'You're from London, Mrs Derby,' Elaine said as the others moved away, and Charlotte nodded.

'Just outside, actually. Do you know London, Miss Mendoza?'

'Do call me Elaine.' The Brazilian girl was insistent. 'And yes, I know London. Papa took me there first when I was just a little girl, and I loved it. All those historic buildings—I expect you're quite used to them.'

'I suppose I am,' murmured Charlotte dryly, and felt unreasonably irritated by the amusement she could see in Logan's face.

'Yes.' Elaine smiled, playing with the zip of her jacket. 'I must get Logan to take me there again some time.'

Charlotte's fingers tightened over the strap of her bag, the urge to score becoming irresistible. 'I should,' she said impulsively. 'He knows the city very well, don't you, Logan?'

The tables were briefly turned, and now Elaine looked irritated. 'You—knew Logan when he was in London, Mrs Derby?' she queried sharply, and Charlotte could feel Logan's keen interest in her reply.

Flushing, she said: 'I—Logan was a—an associate of my husband's, Miss Mendoza. Naturally we met.'

Elaine flicked a glance at the man by her side. 'You didn't tell me you knew Mrs Derby before she came to San Cristobal,' she remarked, the dark eyes flashing. 'When was this?'

Logan looked at Charlotte, and she was appalled at her

own stupidity. Because of Elaine she had placed her whole future in jeopardy. She felt weak with relief when he said carelessly: 'It was all a long time ago, Elaine. Before I began working for your father. When you were still a schoolgirl.'

His use of words was deliberate, but that didn't stop Charlotte from feeling a return of irritation. Did he have to behave as if she was years older than Elaine? There couldn't be more than five or six years between them. But Elaine was clearly pleased with his answer, and the pressure was eased still further when her father appeared.

Charlotte could immediately see why Lisette had been attracted by Manoel Mendoza. Small and dark, like Elaine, he emanated the charm which his daughter possessed in full measure, and his manner was quaintly old-fashioned and courteous. He kissed Charlotte's hand, and his eyes told her that he found her appearance enchanting. It was good to feel attractive again, and she responded to his warmth with more enthusiasm than intelligence. It didn't occur to her that Manoel might misjudge her conduct, and it was potently satisfying to observe Logan's disapproval of her behaviour.

'Have you ever done any underwater swimming, Mrs Derby?' Manoel asked with interest, and Charlotte shook her head.

'No. But I'm—hoping to learn. Perhaps you could teach me, *senhor*.'

'Alas, no.' Manoel nevertheless looked gratified by her suggestion. 'I leave the diving to Logan and Carlos, and Elaine, too, of course. No doubt, she could teach you——'

'I shall be teaching Mrs Derby,' stated Logan with emphasis: 'Shall we go?'

'Where are we going?' asked Charlotte, frowning. Surely it would be more sensible to swim out from the shore, she thought, wishing she had put on her bathing suit before leaving the bungalow.

'We're going to Deadman's Cove!' announced Robert excitedly, appearing at her side. 'Isn't it exciting?'

Charlotte was confused. 'But——' She looked towards the reef. 'How?'

'It's possible to sail the ketch over the reef,' Carlos explained quietly beside her. 'There is a channel that's deep enough to negotiate when the tide is right.'

Charlotte shivered. 'But if we can get out, surely sharks can get in!'

Elaine regarded her scornfully. 'Don't be such a goose, Mrs Derby. There is danger everywhere if you look for it.'

Charlotte's accusing eyes met Logan's. He had already descended the steps to the beach, his arms weighed down with oxygen cylinders, face masks and breathing equipment, and was standing looking up at her. He returned her stare unsmilingly, and then said shortly: 'The chances of a killer shark entering the lagoon are remote, as I said before. Now, can we get going?'

Charlotte glanced round for Robert, but he was already going ahead with Elaine and her father, while Carlos was following them carrying a huge picnic hamper. She wished desperately that she had held out against joining them, or developed a convenient headache this morning. She had imagined they intended staying within the environs of the lagoon, and the idea of sailing to another part of the island filled her with alarm. She was not a good sailor. The trip in the launch from Tortola to San Cristobal had been more than enough for her. Besides, the ketch was smaller than the launch and, in spite of its engine, was basically a sailing vessel.

Carlos turned at the top of the steps and urged her to come along. 'Relax,' he said reassuringly. 'There's no danger.'

'Isn't there?' Charlotte was not convinced. But perhaps that was because her anxieties were not what he imagined them to be.

The ketch rocked beside the landing. Logan and Carlos loaded the diving equipment, and Elaine perched on the gunwale, directing operations. Manoel Mendoza came forward to assist Charlotte, and she was glad of his helping

116

hand as she stepped unsteadily aboard. Robert was stowing the picnic hamper away in a locker, and she thought how much at home he seemed. But then he had been out with Carlos several times already.

The ketch had two masts, but the sails remained furled as Logan used the engine to steer them through the narrow channel into the open sea. The tide was coming in, and the thunderous roar of the surf as it broke along the jaws of the reef, yawning at either side of them, was deafening. Charlotte, seated near the bow of the vessel, clutched the sides of the boat with real terror.

Then they were through, and Elaine and Logan began hauling up the mainsail as Carlos cut the motor. Away from the dangerous crenellations of the reef, Charlotte relaxed a little, and could even respond when Manoel commented on the strength of the wind.

'Do—do you think it's going to be choppy?' she asked, eyeing the white-capped breakers all about them, and he frowned.

'Perhaps, a little. But she can take it.' He patted the side of the ketch. 'It's a good day for sport. Have you done much sailing, Mrs Derby?'

Charlotte shook her head. 'None, I'm afraid. I—boats have never appealed to me.'

'No?' Manoel sounded surprised. 'But you must agree, it is very pleasant to sit here and let the wind carry you where it wills.'

Charlotte forced a smile, trying not to look over the sides of the boat. The idea of being at the mercy of the wind did not appeal to her at all.

Elaine, on the other hand, was obviously enjoying herself immensely. She stood close to Logan, looking up at him through her lustrous almond eyes, and Charlotte couldn't fail to read the message behind the silent display. No wonder Lisette had been so put out by her arrival. Without saying a word, Elaine could convey an unmistakable intimacy.

Robert came to join his mother, grinning happily. 'Isn't

it great!' he exclaimed. 'Carlos let me handle the wheel for a while.'

Manoel smiled at the boy's excited face. 'You do not share your mother's trepidation, Robert?'

'Oh, no.' Robert spread his hands. 'I love it.'

Manoel nodded. 'You are an apt pupil, I am sure.' He looked at Charlotte. 'Did he tell you how Logan was teaching him to use the breathing tube yesterday?'

Remembering how weary and depressed she had been the night before, and how absently she had listened to her son recounting the events of his day, Charlotte had to shake her head, but Robert looked indignant.

'I did tell you, but you weren't listening!' he exclaimed. 'Just from the beach, to begin with. Mr Kennedy let me put on the flippers and face mask, and he swam out with me. He can hold his breath for ever such a long time. He swam underwater part of the way, and he didn't have even a breathing tube.'

Manoel nodded. 'Your son was very good,' he told Charlotte indulgently. 'Logan was very pleased with him.'

Charlotte had the feeling their conversation was being observed, and glancing round she was hardly surprised to find Logan watching them. Standing there, feet apart, braced against the pitching movement of the boat, he looked grim and strangely forbidding. She wondered what it was that was causing that frown of disapproval that tugged down the corners of his mouth, and forced Elaine to look elsewhere for attention.

The Brazilian girl came sauntering across to where her father and Charlotte were sitting, flicking an affectionate smile at Robert. But she was clearly in a mood for argument, and she began by chiding Manoel for wearing trousers instead of shorts, like the other men.

'You are on holiday,' she taunted, speaking English deliberately, Charlotte felt. It could not have missed the other girl's notice that she was wearing trousers, too, and no doubt her comments were double-edged.

'I prefer trousers,' Manoel replied tolerantly. 'I do not

dictate to you what you should wear, Elaine. Surely you can allow me the same privilege.'

Elaine shrugged. That had merely been an opening gambit, Charlotte felt sure.

'Are you enjoying the trip, Mrs Derby?' she asked now, levering her lissom body up on to the engine housing. 'You're looking a little nervous, no?'

Charlotte eased her grip on the bowsprit. 'It's—very pleasant,' she managed jerkily. She looked at Manoel. 'Is—Deadman's Cove much further?'

Robert answered her question: 'Carlos says it takes about three-quarters of an hour,' he declared, arousing her worst fears. They had only been on the water for about fifteen minutes as yet, and already she was feeling slightly queasy. She had deliberately eaten very little for her breakfast, and now the emptiness in her stomach added its own pangs to her discomfort.

Elaine stretched her length so that she could look over the side and into the water. 'You should look down, Mrs Derby,' she said. 'The water's crystal clear. I can see acres of waving grasses, just like the pampas back home. Oh—and what colour the fishes have! Do look, Mrs Derby, it's absolutely fascinating.'

Charlotte turned her head reluctantly, and glanced over the side. All she could see was rolling water, and the rise and fall of the ketch was nauseating. She looked quickly away again, and as she did so, she caught Elaine's eyes upon her. The Brazilian girl turned away, but not before Charlotte had glimpsed the malicious amusement in her face.

Not that Charlotte could have done anything about it right then. Nausea rose like bile in her throat, and she got unsteadily to her feet. She had to get away from people, she thought sickly, realising that Manoel was looking up at her in surprise, and even Robert didn't understand what she was doing.

She had only taken a couple of shaky steps across the planking when Logan's arm encircled her waist, and his support was unexpectedly comforting. 'Cool it!' he advised softly, drawing her across to the wheel. 'Here, hold on to this, and look towards the horizon. Not at the water. Just the horizon.'

Charlotte couldn't have protested, even had she wanted to. But in any case, Logan seemed to know instinctively what was wrong with her. 'I—I feel dreadful,' she confessed, and felt him move to stand behind her, his arm brushing hers as he guided her hands on the wheel.

'Why didn't you tell me you were no sailor?' he demanded beside her ear, and she shivered.

'I—I didn't realise we would be leaving the lagoon. I shouldn't have come.'

'Nonsense!' Logan's voice was hardening again, as if he regretted the sympathy he had shown her. 'We have to conquer these adolescent fears. You're feeling better now, aren't you?'

'A little,' Charlotte had to admit.

'You see?' There was a note of impatience in his tone now, which was not improved by Elaine's decision to join them.

'What's the matter, Mrs Derby?' she inquired mockingly. 'Feeling seasick?'

Charlotte saw no point in deviating. 'Yes,' she said, sensing Logan's hostility, but not understanding it. 'I'm afraid I'd make a poor yachtswoman.'

Elaine pushed her hands into the pockets of her jacket, and looked provocatively at Logan. 'A new role for you, *querido*?' she suggested tauntingly. 'Or perhaps Mrs Derby thought you needed company.'

Charlotte was indignant, but Logan merely pulled a face at Elaine, apparently immune to her malice. '*You* wouldn't do a thing like that, of course,' he jeered, and now Charlotte had the satisfaction of seeing the other girl discomfited.

'People shouldn't come sailing if they can't take it!' she asserted sulkily, and Logan looked amused.

'As I recall, a certain sixteen-year-old lost her stomach off Cape Ignatia some years ago,' he remarked, and she compressed her lips angrily.

'I wasn't seasick!' she declared hotly. 'I wasn't well ...'

'Nor is Charlotte.'

Elaine's lips tightened. 'Mrs Derby looks all right to me.'

Logan sighed. He seemed to be getting bored with the discussion. 'Go and ask Carlos to shorten the mainsheet,' he told her shortly. 'We're tacking too close to the wind. At this rate we'll not make it within the hour.'

Elaine left them with unconcealed reluctance, and Charlotte made an apologetic gesture. 'I—I feel much better now. I'll go and sit down again.'

Logan stepped into her path. 'Beside Mendoza?' he asked harshly, his back towards that gentleman.

Charlotte was forced to delay. 'Why not?'

'I'd rather you didn't sit with Manoel,' he said, surprising her. 'He might—misunderstand your interest.'

Charlotte flushed. 'I don't understand.'

Logan's mouth tightened. 'If you say much more, I shall be forced to draw the conclusion that you prefer older men,' he snapped.

Charlotte gasped. 'What do you mean?'

'Manoel is a widower. His wife died several years ago. For some time now, since Elaine has grown up, he has been hinting that he might marry again. He is a gregarious man, he likes companionship. Naturally, he expects Elaine to get married soon, and when she does ...'

Charlotte was trembling with indignation. 'If you think for one minute——'

'I didn't,' retorted Logan dryly. 'But *he* might.'

'Oh, don't be so silly!' She was hot and embarrassed, as well as resentful. Did he honestly think she might consider remarrying a man only a few years younger than Matthew had been?

'What is so silly?' Logan demanded quietly. 'You did it before.'

Charlotte pressed her palms tightly together. She had spoken recklessly again. 'That—that was different,' she stammered.

121

'How?'

'Logan! We can't talk about this now. Not here!'

'When and where can we talk about it then?' he pursued, coldly. 'You seem singularly unwilling to discuss it at all.'

Charlotte looked about her with some anxiety, sure that their conversation must be audible to other ears as well as their own. But although Carlos and Elaine were looking in their direction, they could not overhear what was being said.

'I don't see that there's anything to talk about,' she said, in an undertone.

'Don't you?' Logan's nostrils flared. 'Your insensitivity is only equalled by your lack of imagination. Don't you think I deserve an explanation? What changed your opinion of Derby? Why did marrying him suddenly prove such an attraction? If it wasn't his money, what was it?'

Charlotte's nervousness manifested itself in her stomach, and the nausea she had felt earlier came back worse than before. 'Oh, please,' she begged. 'Leave me alone!'

Logan's eyes narrowed. 'Are you all right?' he demanded, but she was in no state to answer him.

With a little sob, she rushed to the side, and gave herself up to wretchedness. She heard Robert's worried exclamations mingling with Manoel's concerned reassurances; but it was Logan again who eventually interposed himself between her and the rail, pushing a linen napkin into her hand, and drawing her down on to the rough wooden seating.

She wiped her face miserably, aware of all eyes upon her, Logan's the nearest, and the most inscrutable. 'If this is what happens when I ask what I considered to be a perfectly reasonable question, I shall have to be more careful what I say in future,' he commented dryly.

Charlotte's lips twitched. 'I'm sorry.' She looked down at her pants, their pristine whiteness stained now with the salt water which had splashed over the side. 'What a mess!'

Logan got to his feet. 'A physical or a mental observation?' he queried softly, and then lifted his hand apologetically. 'Don't answer that.'

Carlos was watching them from the wheel. He had apparently taken over in Logan's absence, and his expression was sympathetic. Robert, who had been hovering close by, probably told to keep out of the way until his mother was feeling better, now approached her, his smile anxious.

'Are you okay, Mum?' he exclaimed, and then looked up at Logan. 'Is she?'

Logan inclined his head. 'I think so. Now.'

Robert looked relieved. 'Miss Mendoza said we might have to turn back. But you'll be okay, won't you, Mum?'

Logan's mouth turned down. 'I get the impression you're more concerned on your own behalf than your mother's,' he remarked caustically.

Robert went bright red, unaccustomed to being spoken to in that tone by Logan. 'I'm not!' he muttered defensively. 'I just asked——'

'I know exactly what you asked,' retorted Logan sharply. 'Give a thought to your mother's feelings, can't you? It's not pleasant being made to feel you're in the way!'

'I didn't!'

Robert looked appealingly towards Charlotte, and she took pity on him. 'I really do feel much better, Robert,' she assured him, although in truth she was still uneasy. Her eyes met Logan's. 'Thank you,' she added, and an unreadable expression crossed his face before he strode back to the wheel.

CHAPTER NINE

THEY dropped anchor in Deadman's Cove about twenty minutes later. Charlotte had done as Logan suggested and determinedly kept her eyes on the steady line of the horizon, and by the time they moored in the cove she was able to view her surroundings with more enthusiasm. The waters of the cove were too shallow to sail closer to the beach, she heard Logan explaining to Manoel, but it was possible to swim ashore without difficulty.

It was a little before eleven, and Carlos opened up one of the lockers and extracted cans of lager from a cold box. Manoel decided that he would like coffee instead and Charlotte agreed that she would prefer something non-alcoholic.

'Why is it called Deadman's Cove?' Robert was asking now, and Logan pointed to the steep, tropically foliaged cliff which backed the semi-circle of sand across the remaining expanse of water.

'It's said that pirates used to maroon men here,' he remarked knowledgeably. 'There's no escape. The cliffs are unscalable, and as there is no fresh water supply ...' He grimaced mockingly, his previous impatience with the boy apparently dispersed. 'Make sure you're back on board before we sail!'

Robert grinned, and Charlotte guessed he was relieved to be back on good terms with Logan again. 'I will, don't worry.' He looked over the side. 'Can we swim?'

'That's what we're here for,' declared Elaine irritably, obviously not appreciating being ignored. 'Logan, help me on with this harness. I can't wait to get into the water.'

Logan glanced round at her resignedly, wiping chilled lager from his mouth with the back of his hand. 'Put that cylinder down, Elaine,' he said in much the same tone he

124

had used to Robert earlier. 'If you want to swim, go ahead, but you're not to go diving alone.'

Elaine dropped the cylinder with a thud on to the deck, and Logan's mouth tightened. But he said nothing, merely continued to drink from the can of lager he had opened. Manoel had come to join Charlotte where she was standing near the stern, and he pulled a face at his daughter's show of temper.

'Elaine will learn that she cannot control Logan as she manages to control me,' he observed softly. 'But generally they get along very well, don't you think?'

Charlotte ignored the uncoiling core of jealousy inside her. She had to admit that was what it was, but she also knew she had to overcome it. Even so, Manoel's words, like his daughter's, were chosen for a purpose, and she wasn't altogether sure she liked his way of coupling them together; both parents—but different generations, she thought frustratedly.

Now she sipped the mug of coffee Carlos had given her, and said cautiously: 'I really don't know them—well enough to judge.'

'No, perhaps not.' Manoel was not perturbed. 'But Elaine needs someone like Logan to keep her in order. A weaker man would have the devil's own life with her.'

'As you do?' inquired Charlotte wryly, unable to resist the retort, and he chuckled good-humouredly.

'Indeed. As I do,' he agreed, without rancour.

Logan appeared at her side. 'You are wearing a bathing suit, Charlotte?' he asked curtly, and she turned to him with unwilling eagerness.

'I've—brought a bathing suit,' she admitted reluctantly, 'but I'm not wearing it.'

Logan's irritation was evident. 'You're going to get wet if you don't,' he observed. 'I suggest you change.'

'Here?' Charlotte was horrified. 'Now!'

'As soon as Carlos and the others are in the water, yes.' He turned to her companion. 'Manoel, I have something I'd like you to see.'

The two men moved away together and Charlotte looked round frustratedly. Elaine had apparently taken Logan at his word, and she and Robert were already in the water. The Brazilian girl had shed her cotton jacket and the bra of her bikini was as scanty as the briefs.

Carlos was preparing to use a snorkel. He had already put on the face mask and was adjusting the breathing tube before lowering himself into the water. Rubber flippers flapped noisily as he stepped over the side, and he raised a hand in salute to Logan as he disappeared.

Charlotte sighed. Three down and two to go, she thought irritably. How could she get changed here? It was far too exposed. She had expected to be able to change in Logan's bungalow, not on the deck of the sailboat.

Logan turned from the chart he had spread out on the engine housing and which he and Manoel had been studying to regard her impatiently.

'You can go ahead,' he remarked. 'Get changed! I promise we won't look.'

Charlotte's face burned. 'I don't think I want to go in the water,' she said.

Logan's mouth compressed. 'Don't be foolish, Charlotte. That's the whole point of the exercise.'

'Your exercise, perhaps,' she replied, speaking as pleasantly as she could, aware of Manoel watching their exchange. 'I—really, I'm fine——'

'Charlotte!' Logan's voice had that harsh ring about it now, but Manoel intervened.

'I think perhaps—Charlotte? May I?' He smiled ingenuously; 'I think perhaps Charlotte would prefer to be completely alone, Logan. That's understandable, isn't it? Come.' He began to unfasten his trousers, and Charlotte's momentary fears were stilled when they revealed navy blue swimming trunks beneath. 'I shall enjoy a swim myself.'

Logan's smouldering stare moved from Charlotte to the other man. He seemed about to make some further comment, but changed his mind at the last minute. With a brief word, which even someone who did not understand his language could apprehend as being far from complimentary, he folded the chart, thrust it away in a locker and accompanied Manoel to the rail. But when the older man performed a neat dive into the lucid green waters of the cove, he stepped back again and Charlotte was confronted by his tight-lipped disapproval.

'Such a fuss!' he snapped sharply. 'You really do enjoy annoying me, don't you?'

Charlotte held up her head. 'Just because I'm not prepared to do a striptease for your benefit——'

'A striptease!' Logan was scathing. 'I doubt if you'd know how.' Then, as she recoiled from him, he added: 'Do you want me to take your clothes off myself?'

She gasped, but now was not the time for trepidation. 'Oh, yes,' she exclaimed. 'You'd enjoy that, wouldn't you? No doubt you've had plenty of experience!'

'With you?' His lips twisted. 'Not as much as I'd like, believe me!'

Charlotte's brief spasm of aggression was rendered useless. However she tried to fight him, he had an innate ability to disarm her.

'So?' he went on. 'Must we waste any more time?'

Charlotte's fingers moved obediently to the tied fastening beneath her breasts. The tapes pulled loose quite easily, but she held them in her hands, keeping the two sides of the blouse in position. For a moment Logan seemed mesmerised by her actions, and then with a muffled oath, he turned away, vaulting over the gunwale and into the water without a backward glance.

Charlotte's two-piece bathing suit could hardly be called a bikini, but she had lost weight since coming to San Cristobal, and the belted briefs hung low on her slender hips. The bra fitted better, its cleavage exposing the swelling contours of creamy white skin. She removed the chiffon scarf which confined her hair, and immediately the weight of honey-brown hair tumbled about her shoulders. She thought how wet it would become in the water, and guessed

127

that was why Elaine wore such an easy-to-manage style.

Robert's hands came to grip the side of the boat, and the top of his head appeared. 'Are you coming in the water— *hey*! You look super, Mum!'

Far from reassuring her, Robert's words made her doubtful. 'I might just sunbathe——' she was beginning, when Carlos swung himself back on board.

'You ready, Mrs Derby?' he inquired easily, and with a sigh, she nodded.

Carlos's gleaming black body dripped water over the bleached boards of the ketch as he handed her a pair of flippers and told her to put them on her feet.

'Have you ever swum with rubbers?' he asked, and she shook her head. 'You'd better get used to them first, then,' he suggested, and she stood looking at him doubtfully, feeling ridiculously like a stranded penguin.

'What do I do?'

'Well, you get in the water,' he told her dryly. 'Do you need any assistance?'

'Oh, no. No!' She shook her head, and under Robert's amused stare, she clambered over the side and practically tumbled head-first into the soft clear water.

It was difficult surfacing. Her feet kept wanting to be where her head should be, and she realised what Carlos had meant about getting used to the flippers. She came up spluttering to find Logan beside her, and he grasped a painful handful of her hair to keep her afloat. Her eyes stung, but he seemed immune to her discomfort.

'Kick your legs,' he told her. 'That's right. Not too hard. Get a rhythm, and you'll find it's easy.'

And it was—but Charlotte was more conscious of his nearness than anything else. She stared at him tormentedly and when he released her hair to turn her back to him, his hand firm on her midriff, she thought he had guessed what she was thinking.

But when his name spilled from her lips, he merely tightened his hold on her, saying half impatiently: 'Kick your legs and let your body relax. Now, can you hold your breath for a while, and I'll show you how to keep just below the surface of the water?'

Despite Elaine's chiding ridicule and Robert's well-meaning interference, Charlotte soon mastered the technique of allowing her legs to propel her forward. Instead of threshing about wildly with her arms and defeating her object, she learned to keep them by her sides, and glide smoothly through the water. This achieved, Logan taught her how to open her eyes underwater, and the sun-warmed world which opened up beneath her displaced all lingering traces of self-consciousness.

She had been afraid she might feel sick, as she had in the boat, but there was so much to see she forgot to even think about it. The water wasn't deep, no more than six to eight feet, but it teemed with life. Waving banks of turtle grass gave way to rocky formations, where every crack and cranny harboured sponges and sea urchins, snails and anemones, and small corals clinging for survival. She had imagined the colours would be muted, but she sunlight was so strong, the patterns of the vivid creatures they passed stood out in bright relief. There were tropical fish of every kind, as well as worms and starfish, and armoured shell-fish that withdrew inside their defences with the touch of a finger.

As soon as Logan was satisfied she was at home in the water, he swam back to the boat and collected her a face mask and snorkel, introducing her to the technique of breathing through a tube. The mouthpiece seemed huge to begin with, but Logan was patient and soon she could handle it without choking.

'Are you going to spend the whole day playing about in the shallows?' Elaine was demanding of Logan, when Charlotte emerged from an exhilarating spell in the cathedral quiet below the surface, and he shook his head.

'Once Charlotte has mastered using the snorkel, we'll go out into deeper water,' he promised her indulgently, and Charlotte guessed he meant to use the oxygen tanks.

'Don't concern yourself about me,' she said at once, pushing the mask up over her hair. 'Robert and I can manage quite satisfactorily on our own.'

Logan's reaction was not entirely unexpected. 'I shall decide if or when you can satisfactorily be left alone,' he stated, raking back his wet hair. Unlike her, he had not worn a mask and breathing tube, relying instead on his experienced control of his breathing, surfacing only to fill his lungs before plunging underwater once more. 'And as it is after twelve, I suggest we have lunch before venturing further afield.'

It was too hot to put on any clothes, and Charlotte contented herself with the thought that so long as Elaine was around, no one would pay much attention to her. That she was wrong soon became obvious when Manoel insinuated himself beside her, although it crossed her mind that Elaine might be encouraging her father's interest, pairing off Carlos with Robert, and herself with Logan.

Lunch was a delicious meal of cold chicken and potato salad, ham rolls, lettuce, tomatoes, and cheese. There were lobster patties, and mushroom *vol-au-vents*, savoury sausages and stuffed eggs, as well as cherry meringues and chocolate icecream, that melted before it was consumed. There was plenty of fresh fruit for those who wanted it and two bottles of champagne, which Manoel confided he had provided. It was delightful relaxing after the morning's activities, and in a facile way, Charlotte was enjoying herself. It was strange to think that until recently she had found nothing unusual in spending a whole day in idleness, when now, after only a little under three weeks, she already appreciated the privilege.

Logan lounged on the deck with Carlos, while Elaine stretched her length beside them, lying on her stomach and unfastening the bikini bra so that the heat of the sun should not leave a mark across her already bronzed back. Charlotte was dismayed at her own reactions to this deliberate display of provocation, but she was unaware she was staring until Logan intercepted her gaze and shrewdly guessed the reason for it. The palm of his hand descended on Elaine's smooth flesh, and Charlotte was hotly resentful when what he said drifted easily on the still air:

'I think you had better make yourself decent, *pequena*. You are embarrassing my guest.'

Immediately, Elaine sat up and looked defiantly across at Charlotte, making no attempt to cover herself. 'What is the matter, Mrs Derby?' she demanded carelessly. 'Haven't you ever gone—how do you say it?—topless, no?'

Robert's reactions were to gather up some shells he had collected and carry them to the rear end of the boat, but before Charlotte could make any protest, Logan thrust a towel into Elaine's unwilling hands.

'That will do,' he told her flatly, and she made an angry face at him before pushing the towel aside and snatching up the bra and putting it on again.

'Such a fuss!' she muttered sulkily. 'No one else is complaining. Just because she's a prude——'

'*Caluda!*' Logan lapsed into Portuguese, and judging from Elaine's expression, Charlotte did not think that what he was saying was particularly favourable to her. Manoel raised his eyebrows, but made no complaint, and with a pang she realised that he was prepared to countenance Logan's censure because he approved of their relationship.

After a while they all relaxed, physically at least, although Charlotte's mind was far from inactive. She contemplated Logan through half closed lids, relieved to see that his eyes were closed. He was lying flat on his back and her eyes moved over his supine form, lingering on the taut skin covering his rib-cage, his flat stomach, and the powerful muscles of his thighs. His legs were long and darkened with hair, his feet narrow and well formed. She gained a certain amount of satisfaction from the knowledge that Robert had inherited his father's lithe indolence, and in a few years would no doubt be equally attractive to the opposite sex. Even so, it was incredible to think that she and Logan had once shared such an intimacy, had once lain in one another's arms without even the barrier of a bathing suit between them. And yet was it so incredible, when only days ago she had experienced a similarly wanton sensation on the beach?

Elaine was lying beside him, and every now and then she inched a little nearer to him, and Charlotte, suppressing her real feelings, turned her head to look at her son. Unlike the others, he was not sleeping. On his stomach, he was examining a snail he had found, intent on the fluted formation of its shell. He looked so much like Logan at that moment that she glanced round almost guiltily, sure that her secret must be evident to all eyes. But fortunately, no one else was looking at him just then, and she expelled her breath on a sigh.

Observing Robert brought other considerations to mind, and she tried to put her mind to sorting out what she would do when this month was up. She would go back to London, of course, that much seemed certain. It would be easier to lose herself there, and there was bound to be some kind of employment she could take up. Robert was a problem, but not an insurmountable one. If it was at all possible, she would find another housekeeping position where Robert's presence would not be frowned upon, but if not, he was old enough to be left alone during school holidays and such like.

Just for a moment she allowed herself to imagine what their life might have been like if Logan had not abandoned her, if they had got married, and Robert had been born out of love and not bitterness. She wondered if she would have liked living in Rio, and then chided herself for her foolishness. She could have been happy anywhere with the man she loved, and Logan had always been that man. Even now ...

She had not been aware of Logan moving, and when his weight was suddenly lowered beside hers, she looked up at him in alarm.

'Relax,' he told her softly, indicating Manoel's sleeping form. 'I just want to talk to you.'

Charlotte glanced anxiously towards Robert, but he had shifted so that his back was to them, and as even Elaine

132

seemed unconscious of Logan's departure, they seemed suddenly isolated.

'Wh-what do you want to talk about?' she ventured.

Logan's arm rested along the back of the seat behind her. 'Us,' he answered quietly.

Charlotte pressed a hand to her throat. 'Us?' she echoed.

'Yes, us. You and me—and Robert.'

After her thoughts of the last few minutes, his words were too perceptive, and in an effort to avoid a direct answer, she exclaimed: 'I have no intention of staying on with Lisette after the month is up, so there's no point in you——'

'Did I say I wanted you to stay on with Lisette?' he interrupted her harshly, and she coloured.

'No ...'

'So don't jump to conclusions.'

'I'm sorry.'

'Oh, Charlotte!' His use of her name was frustrated. Then, as if aware that they might be overheard, he went on more evenly: 'What do you think of San Cristobal?'

Charlotte was surprised, and a little disappointed by his question. 'I—it's all right,' she replied.

'Is that all? All right? Don't you think it's a beautiful island?'

Charlotte hesitated. 'Yes, it's beautiful,' she agreed at last without enthusiasm.

Logan heaved a sigh. 'Don't overdo it!' he remarked. 'I might get the wrong impression.'

'You asked me what I thought of the island and——'

'—and you told me. Yes.' Logan paused. 'What about Robert?'

'What about Robert?'

'Is he happy here? Or is he bored?'

Charlotte looked down at her toes. 'You must know that since he started visiting the beach house, he's been in seventh heaven!' she told him, half resentfully.

'And that annoys you?' he demanded, in an undertone.

133

'That Matthew's son enjoys my company? And Carlos's too, of course.'

Charlotte refused to meet his gaze. 'I—no. Why should it?'

'That's what I ask myself—but it seems to.'

She sighed. 'You're imagining things.'

'Am I?' His fingers touched her bare arm, trailing a path from her wrist to her shoulder. 'Would you like to hear what I do imagine?' He bent his head deliberately so that his breath was fanning her cheek. 'I imagine you in my bed every morning. I imagine I am the only man who has ever possessed you. And I imagine Robert is my son!'

Charlotte had to steel herself not to spring to her feet and put the width of the deck between them. Why was he saying these things to her? Did he suspect something? Or was this just another of his ways to torment her?

'You—you seem to have a vivid imagination,' she managed, at length. 'No doubt you always did.'

'What's that supposed to mean?'

She shivered. 'I see no point in re-hashing old scores, Logan.'

'Don't you? Why not? I should have thought you owed me that, at least.'

'*I owe you!*' She stared at him then, ignoring the assiduous temptation to lift her hand and touch his face, so close to hers. 'Your arrogance is incredible!'

'Why? Because I made love to you?' Logan's fingers insinuated themselves beneath the strap of her bra. 'As a married woman of some eleven years, you're not still harbouring grudges about that!'

Charlotte shifted her shoulder irritably, but it didn't dislodge his probing fingers. 'You would consider that ridiculous, wouldn't you?' she snapped, endeavouring to control emotions that were threatening to get out of hand.

He bent his head, his teeth catching the lobe of her ear. 'You were untouched—I had no right to do it,' he conceded, no doubt aware of the trembling flesh beneath his lips. 'But what you did was worse—and I see no reason to

134

apologise for what was undeniably a delightful experience.'
His fingers caught her chin, turning her face to his.
'Wasn't it?' he insisted, the sensual curve of his mouth
awakening all the wanton desires she had so long suppressed.

'You—you're completely amoral, do you know that?' she
cried, trying to push his hands away, and his expression
changed.

'If we're talking about character references, there was
nothing particularly moral about marrying a man old
enough to be your grandfather, was there?' he drawled
coldly. 'Derby was determined to get his hands on you,
one way or the other, but I never thought you'd let yourself be *bought*! How mistaken I was!'

Charlotte put both hands to her hot cheeks. Elaine was
stirring, disturbed no doubt by the angry tenor of Logan's
voice, but for a few moments longer they were unobserved.

'I don't know why you keep bringing this up,' she said
carefully, ignoring the craving to justify herself. 'As a
matter of fact, I married Matthew because *I* owed *him*, not
the other way about.'

Logan's eyes narrowed. 'What did you owe him?'

Charlotte shifted uncomfortably. 'I—surely that's obvious! He—I—without him, I'd have been brought up in a
children's home.'

'No great hardship, I should have thought.'

'You don't understand, do you?' she exclaimed painfully.

He shook his head. 'No. Unless ...' His eyes were
frankly assessing as they moved over her scantily-clad figure.
'Unless ... the real thing was too much for you.'

'What do you mean?'

'God help me, I don't know,' he muttered angrily,
pushing back his hair with a careless gesture. 'I've tried
to work it out. I've lain awake nights trying to understand
why you did it, and even now, I'm no further forward. God,
Charlotte, you had Robert! You must have slept with him!
Oh——' With a stifled oath, he got to his feet and left her,

135

walking towards Carlos with a curious lack of vitality in his step.

During the afternoon Logan, Carlos and Elaine put on the scuba-diving equipment and somersaulted off the boat to explore the deeper waters that lay at the base of the cliffs that formed the headlands on either side of the cove. Robert was disappointed that he was not allowed to join in such an expedition, but Charlotte comforted him with the suggestion that they should swim to the shore, which was as yet unexplored.

It was further than Charlotte had anticipated, and she was tired when they finally walked up the unblemished stretch of beach. The sand was a dazzling oyster white, disturbed only by delves here and there, which she guessed had been made by crabs or some other sea creature.

While she stretched out to sunbathe, Robert sauntered off to explore, and the peaceful isolation soon made her drowsy. The only sounds came from the seabirds crying overhead, their raucousness muted by distance. The silky lap of the water as it creamed on the shoreline was soothing, and she felt her eyes closing almost against her will.

When she awoke, it was to the discomfiting realisation that she had been too long in the sun. Her arms and legs were bright red and painful to touch, and she dreaded to think what her nose must be like.

She got quickly to her feet, momentarily dizzy as the sea cast back its brilliance in a thousand blinding prisms. She blinked, trying to see more clearly, and was relieved when her vision began to clear.

Only then did she look about her. Where was Robert? How long had she slept? If only she had a watch to give her some indication of the time. The sun was lower, it was true, but not so low that she could imagine she had slept longer than an hour. An hour! She looked down at her limbs exasperatedly. So much damage could be done in an hour, and after all she had said to Robert about guarding against sunburn, she had to go and do something foolish like this!

But where was Robert? She looked all about her, and felt a stirring sense of panic at the realisation that he was not in sight. But then, she told herself impatiently, he would hardly be standing about waiting for her to notice him. Knowing Robert, he was likely to be among that tangle of bushes bordering the cliffs, searching for some shells or rock samples, or simply playing a game of hide and seek with her.

Brushing the sand from her arms and legs with careful fingers, wincing as her muscles objected to the unnatural dryness of her skin, she turned and began to walk up the beach. It was quite steep, due no doubt to the shelving of the cove, and she was almost unaware of a huge sand-crab until it scuttled out from beneath her feet, startling a shocked gasp from her lips. She took a moment to gather her composure, and used the time to call Robert's name.

There was no answer and with some misgivings she pushed between the corrugated trunks of a clump of palm trees. Insects whirred noisily about her, protesting at being disturbed, and her bare feet probed every inch of sand before setting down. There could well be spiders and scorpions lurking among the greenery, and she called Robert's name again, more aggressively this time.

It suddenly occurred to her that he might have swum back to the boat, and reaching the cliff face she was about to give up the search when she saw the wide crack in the rock wall. Curiosity made her go on until she could see through the crack, and she frowned into the cave beyond. Sunlight shafted through the opening, but beyond the circle of illumination was a shadowy interior, echoing to the hollow sound of the sea. Perhaps some cavern lay beneath the cliffs, some underground chamber worn into the solid wall of rock by the ocean.

'Robert?' she called, taking a tentative step through the cleft, refusing to think about spouts and pot-holes, and bottomless wells. 'Are you there, Robert?'

There was no reply, and she was about to abandon the

search, realising there was little she could do without a torch, when she heard a curious cry, not unlike that of a child in distress. Immediately she turned back, staring helplessly into the dim recesses of the cave.

'Robert?' she said again, more urgently now. 'Robert, is that you?'

The muted thunder of the ocean masked any response, but she sensed rather than heard that something was moving about in the darkness beyond her sight.

'Robert!' Her utterance of his name was anxious. 'Robert, can't you answer me?'

There was no further sound and she looked back desperately over her shoulder. Oh, for a match, she thought despairingly, wondering whether it was possible for Robert to have gone into the cave and injured himself in some way. She knew the most sensible course of action was to swim back to the boat and enlist Manoel's help, but the idea of leaving the boy if he was there filled her with reluctance.

She stepped further into the cave, trying to adjust her eyes to the gloom and succeeded in glimpsing the shadowy wall at the back. There seemed to be something lying on the floor of the cave and convinced it must be Robert, she rushed towards it, only to be thrown backward aghast, as a thousand stars exploded inside her head.

CHAPTER TEN

She came to with a thumping headache making itself felt along the hairline of her scalp. She lifted a trembling hand to her forehead, and although the lump she found there was painful, she was relieved to find that apparently there was no blood. But although the temperature in the cave was chilling her legs and arms were stinging, and their discomfort reminded her of her reasons for being where she was.

With a hand raised to ward off any blow, she struggled into a sitting position, and stared across the palely sanded floor towards the back wall of the cave. Whatever had been lying there appeared to have gone, and she tipped back her head to see what had caused the blow to her head.

With eyes fully adjusted to the gloom, it was possible to see the jutting overhang into which she had charged, and observing its rugged exterior, she thought she was lucky not to have concussion. Now, all she felt was a little sick, but that would pass with the headache, no doubt.

She shook her head wearily, and rolled on to her knees, turning towards the brilliant shaft of sunlight still pouring through the cleft in the rock. Obviously, Robert was not here, and somehow she had to get back to the boat and find out exactly where he was. But she didn't honestly know if she had the strength ...

She got unsteadily to her feet and as she did so, the shuffling sound she had heard before came again. Shakily she turned in the direction of the sound, and gulped as a huge grey crab came zig-zagging towards her, its pincer-like claws extended.

It was too much. With a sob, Charlotte stumbled across the uneven floor of the cave, emerging into the sunlight just as Logan came pushing his way through the trees, his face white and tense with some emotion she was too distressed to identify. She ran straight towards him, not caring at that moment how he might construe her actions, just needing the reassurance of his arms about her.

There was a moment when she thought he was going to push her away from him, but then his hands descended on her shoulders, and he jerked her towards him, her overheated flesh welcoming the cool dampness of his. His thumbs massaging her neck, he spoke with evident difficulty: 'Where the hell have you been? Haven't you heard us calling you?'

'No. No.' She moved her head helplessly from side to side, glancing back apprehensively over her shoulder, almost as if she expected the crab to leap on her from behind, and Logan saw the swelling just below her hairline.

'*Dio!*' he muttered savagely. 'What has happened? How did you hurt your head?' Then, more perceptively: 'What are you afraid of?'

Charlotte pressed her face against his chest, and he seemed to become aware of the burning flesh beneath his fingers. With a muffled oath he relaxed the pressure of his hold, staring down at her with a mixture of anger and compassion.

'How in God's name have you got yourself into this state?' he demanded huskily. 'Charlotte, don't you know when I found you were missing, I nearly went out of my mind.'

Charlotte tipped back her head to look at him. 'I—I was looking for Robert,' she breathed, and he briefly closed his eyes.

'Robert's on the boat,' he told her quietly. 'Duly chastened, I might add. Where were you?'

Charlotte quivered. 'In the cave—there.' She nodded back over her shoulder. 'I—I heard a sound.'

'What sort of sound?'

'Like a child crying.' She shook her head again. 'I—I was sure it was him. Then—then I hit my head, and—ugh!' she shuddered uncontrollably.

140

'What? What was it?'

Logan shook her gently, and she forced herself to go on:
'It was a crab, I think. It—it seemed to be coming for
me ...'

'Oh, Charlotte!' His hands tightened agonisingly for a
moment, then he put her aside and strode towards the cleft
in the cliff face. She hung back when he stepped into the
aperture, but at his call she re-entered the cave, reaching
out a cautious hand towards him.

He took her hand and drew her to his side, and as her
eyes accustomed themselves to the light again, he pointed
to what now appeared to be a pile of feathers at the back of
the cave.

'I think you disturbed a ghost crab,' he told her gently.
'What you probably heard was the cry of a bird, a fledgling
perhaps fallen from its nest, and dragged in here by the crab
you saw.'

'Oh, God!' Charlotte was horrified, but Logan made a
resigned gesture. 'It's all part of the pattern,' he told her
wryly. 'The sea-birds steal the turtle's eggs, and the turtle
has no means of defending them.'

'Even so ...'

Charlotte's fingers tightened round his, and he looked
down at her in the gloom. 'Even so ... what? Would you
deny the crab its existence? Don't you think it has as much
right as anything else to survival? Just because it's not as
pretty as the fledgling, does that mean it forfeits its chance
to live?'

'No ...' Charlotte trembled. 'It just seems so—barbaric.'

'It is. But then isn't everything?' he remarked bitterly.
'Not least the woman I loved marrying someone else!'

She would have stepped away from him then, but his
fingers were gripping hers and short of prising them apart,
she could not escape him. 'No, Charlotte,' he said definitely, 'not yet. Do you realise this is the first time we've
been alone together—really alone—since you came here?
Oh, there was that interlude on the beach, but you were too
conscious of prying eyes——'

'Robert was watching us,' she exclaimed tremulously.

'Was he?' Logan raised dark eyebrows. 'I must have a few words with that young man.'

'Don't——'

'Why not? It's time he learned a few home truths. Like who his father was, for example!'

Charlotte stopped struggling. 'Wh-what do you mean?'

Logan's eyes were penetratingly intent. 'Don't you think this has gone on long enough?' he demanded fiercely. 'When do you intend to tell me that Robert is *my* son?'

Charlotte's legs almost sagged beneath her. 'Wh-what?' she gasped, striving for self-control, and his hands curved round her throat, imprisoning her without effort.

'Why do you think I was away so long?' he demanded harshly. 'What do you think I was doing? As soon as I saw him, I knew I was right. I'm a biologist, Charlotte. Genetics is my business. Did you think I couldn't see the resemblance right away? I just had to confirm some dates, that's all. So long as you weren't sleeping with Derby before your marriage, Robert has to be my son.'

Charlotte couldn't seem to stop herself from shaking. It was the reaction, of course; that, and the scalp-jolting blow to her head. *Logan knew!* After all these days of apprehension and anxiety, he knew, and she had had no part in his enlightenment.

Licking dry lips, she got out chokily: 'So? So—what do you intend to do now?'

Logan's eyes darkened. 'I gave you every opportunity. I wanted you to tell me. This afternoon, on the boat—I was sure you would. But you didn't.'

Charlotte managed to turn her head towards the sunlight outside this gloomy cavern, aware of an awful premonition that they were being observed. 'W-won't whoever was with you be wondering where you are?' she cried, sucking in her breath as his fingers tightened convulsively.

'Carlos is searching the headland,' he told her grimly. 'He can stand to suffer a few more minutes—as I have done.'

Charlotte bent her head, and then quickly lifted it again

as her chin touched his hands. 'Logan, what do you want from me? What do you want me to say?'

'I want the truth!' he snapped. 'Did you only marry Derby because you were expecting a child?'

Charlotte stared up at him helplessly. How could she answer him? If she admitted marrying Matthew because of Robert, surely she was jeopardising her own part in his future. If Logan could prove that, then even now he stood a chance of gaining control of the boy. After all, what did she have to offer him compared to Logan? She had no home, no money—and probably now, no employment either. Whatever he said, nothing could alter the fact that he had seduced her and left her without even bothering to find out whether she was all right. He had known she was a virgin. His insensitivity at that time could never be justified. and if he now found the idea of having a son appealing, he should marry Elaine and produce a family of his own. At this point her nerve gave out on her. It was one thing to justify what she had done, but quite another to accept comparable behaviour from him ...

'All right,' she said unevenly. 'I was—I was pregnant when I married Matthew, but that wasn't why I married him.'

Logan's jaw was hard. 'No?'

'No.' She could feel a revealing nerve in her chin jerking, and was briefly glad of the dimness in the cave. 'I—we—Matthew cared about me, and I—I cared for him——'

She broke off chokingly as his thumb pressed hard on her windpipe. 'I don't believe it,' he muttered savagely. 'I won't believe it. Charlotte, for God's sake, show some compassion!'

'As you did?' she managed to articulate. 'Taking advantage of a young girl—knowing she had no experience in such thing' You didn't care, did you? Just so long as you were satisfied' How many other girls enjoyed the privilege, I wonder' How many other casual affairs did you have?'

'No others!' he ground out the words. 'Charlotte, I loved you——'

143

'Love? Is that what you call it?' Her words were finding their target, that much she guessed from his weakening grip on her throat, and she pressed home her advantage. 'The only person you care about is yourself. Self-gratification, that's what we're talking about. That's why you needed to know Robert was your son, didn't you? Because it hurt your pride to think that I might have found happiness with some other man, particularly a man you despised!'

There was silence for a few seconds, and then Logan's hands fell to his sides. 'I can see I'm wasting my time,' he said heavily. 'If that's what you think, then there's nothing more to be said.'

Charlotte put a hand to her sore throat. Why was it whenever he attacked her, she always emerged feeling the guilty one? Unable to prevent herself, she asked: 'What—what will you do?'

Logan's eyes narrowed. 'What will I do?'

'Yes.' She linked her fingers together. 'A-about Robert?'

'What do you expect me to do?'

'Logan, for pity's sake! You know what I mean.'

He rubbed the back of his neck with a weary hand. 'I suppose now it's my turn to keep you in suspense, isn't it?' he considered. 'Why should I make it easy for you? What have I to gain? He is my son, isn't he?'

A sob rose in her throat and escaped on a sigh. 'Oh, Logan ...' she whispered despairingly, and as if he couldn't bear her distress, he retorted violently: 'Don't worry. I shan't say anything, if that's what you're afraid of. If you see no reason to tell Robert the truth, I can't force you. You'll be leaving in a little over a week, won't you? Then you can relax in the knowledge that we won't ever see one another again.'

Charlotte pressed her fingertips to her lips, looking up at him through a mist of tears. Why didn't he ever conform to her preconceived expectations of him? If only he had gone on reviling her, hurting her, making her despise him for his arrogance, instead of withdrawing from the contest, leaving her with this overwhelming awareness of his vulnerability.

She shivered. The cave was cold, but before she left this place there was one more thing she had to know. 'Robert ...' she began unevenly. 'Is he—do you—what do you think of him?'

She was unprepared for the look of anguish that crossed his face. 'My God,' he muttered bitterly, 'you do demand your pound of flesh, don't you?'

With a rough oath, he would have brushed past her, but she put out her hand and stopped him, her fingers encountering the cooling flesh of his forearm. 'Logan ...' she began distractedly, and as he halted, reached up involuntarily and stroked his taut cheek.

He turned to look at her then, but now her eyes dropped to the low waistband of his shorts, and she withdrew her hands, pressing them to her middle. 'I'm sorry.'

He did not move away, however. Instead, he took her hands and drew them to his body. 'Touch me!' he commanded, in a tortured voice. '*Hold me!* Oh, God, I *need* you!'

Her lids lifted and her eyes encountered his scorching gaze. She was no longer conscious of the chilling atmosphere around them, only of what this man was asking of her, and what she was prepared to give. His hungry mouth sought and found hers, and her lips parted without thought of denial, until she felt she was drowning in sensual feeling. She made no protest when the fastening on her bra was released, and his hands caressing and squeezing the hardening nipples of her breasts were frankly arousing. His hands slid over her hips, compelling her closer, and her softness crushed against him evoked his muffled groan.

'You ask me what I think of my son, and then do this to me,' he protested unsteadily. 'Charlotte, I——'

'*Tu bastardo!*'

Charlotte did not need an understanding of Portuguese to translate the words, but that they were uttered by Elaine Mendoza caused her to drag herself away from Logan, turning to stare in shocked fascination at the Brazilian girl. She was standing in the cleft of the rock wall, arms folded, the belt she had worn to support the oxygen tank still suspended from her waist.

'So you do not always—how do you say it?—practise what you condemn, Mrs Derby,' she sneered. 'I guessed you would take off your clothes for Logan, if he invited you to.'

Horrified, Charlotte realised what she meant, and spread her arms cross-wise in a vain attempt to cover herself. Logan, grim and tight-lipped, rescued her bra from the floor of the cave where it had fallen, and thrust it bleakly into her hand, putting himself between her and Elaine, seemingly uncaring what the younger girl thought of him.

'Did you want something?' he inquired curtly, and Charlotte heard Elaine's indignant intake of air.

'You were missing so long, I thought you might be hurt,' she declared jerkily.

'So you came looking for me?'

'Yes.'

'Where is Carlos?'

Elaine shrugged indifferently. 'How should I know?'

'Did he swim back to the boat?'

'Not yet.' Elaine clenched her fists. 'He's on the beach, if you must know.'

'He told you where I was?'

Charlotte could feel the other girl's discomfort, but couldn't understand it.

'I—not exactly,' Elaine muttered now. 'But you were missing, and—and so was *she*! Carlos's eyes are very expressive.'

Charlotte came from behind Logan, combing her hands through her hair. 'Carlos knew where we were?' she echoed, forgetting for a moment to whom she was speaking, and then remembered that moment when she had sensed those unseen eyes. She turned accusingly to Logan 'He *knew*?'

Logan gave her a hard-eyed stare. 'He wasn't watching us, if that's what you're implying,' he retorted. 'Like me, he knew this cave was here. When he heard our voices, he went away again.'

Charlotte pressed the palms of her hands to her hot cheeks, and as if on cue, Elaine stepped aside so that she could emerge into the sunlight once more.

It was a relief to feel the warmth of the sun on her chilled limbs, but the sensation was only momentary before the results of her earlier exposure began to protest. Logan followed the two girls outside, and at once he guessed why Charlotte was endeavouring to cover her arms with her hands.

'Your burns!' he muttered impatiently. 'Dear God, Charlotte, how did it happen? Don't you have any more sense than to——'

'I fell asleep,' she told him shortly, realising they were both suffering the after-effects of overcharged emotions. 'I'll put some lotion on when I get—back.'

She had almost said home, but Avocado Cay could never be home to her.

'I have some cream on the boat,' stated Logan grimly. 'I'll get Carlos to attend to it.'

'Don't bother.' Charlotte was finding it incredibly difficult to behave naturally, particularly as Elaine seemed unwilling to drag her eyes away from her. 'I can manage.'

She began to walk away, but Logan came after her, his hand around her arm causing her to wince with pain. His brows drew together as he realised what was wrong, but apart from that brief acknowledgment, he made no attempt to loosen his grip.

'Charlotte,' he exclaimed, glancing back over his shoulder at Elaine. 'We haven't finished.'

'Again?' As her blood cooled, common sense was taking over, and Charlotte was horrified by the realisation that if Elaine had not interrupted them, she would have been powerless to prevent him from taking her—there, on the floor of the cave. It had always been like that with him, she remembered bitterly, loathing her own body that could betray her so recklessly. 'I have.'

'Charlotte!' His expression was tormented. 'Listen to me!'

'Not now, Logan.' There was a burning sensation at the backs of her eyes, and she knew that tears were not far away. But she refused to cry in front of Elaine. That would be the final humiliation.

'All right. He let her go and she wrapped tentative fingers round the marks he had left on her scorched flesh. He gave Elaine an unsmiling look. 'We can't talk now, I agree. Later.'

Charlotte stumbled on without answering him, and emerged from the trees to find Carlos standing waiting for them, his face mirroring his anxiety. When he saw Charlotte's injuries, however, his expression changed, and he came towards her swiftly, exclaiming at the purple lump on her head.

'What did you do?' he cried, but Logan reached them and brushed his questions aside.

'Not yet, Carlos,' he insisted grimly. 'Somehow we've got to get her out to the ketch.'

'I can swim,' exclaimed Charlotte indignantly, but Logan ignored her.

'Is that rubber dinghy still on board?' he asked, and when Carlos agreed that it was, he strode away down the beach, wading into the water and swimming strongly out towards the boat.

After a moment's hesitation, Elaine ran after him, her shorter strokes taking her quickly through the water so that she climbed aboard only a couple of minutes after he did.

Charlotte sank down weakly on to the sand, too distraught to protest any further, and Carlos squatted sympathetically beside her. 'You all right, Mrs Derby?' he asked anxiously, and she forced a slight smile.

'What do they say?' She tried to make light of it. 'As well as can be expected in the circumstances?' She lifted her stiff shoulders. 'I've been a fool, Carlos. In more ways than one.'

'We all make mistakes sometimes.' Carlos frowned. 'I'm sorry I couldn't stop Miss Mendoza from disturbing you.'

'You're sorry!' Charlotte's laugh was slightly hysterical. 'Well, don't be. She came—just in time.'

Carlos looked down at the fine sand, scuffing it with his bare toes. 'Mrs Derby, I don't know how to say this——'

'Then don't try!' She didn't want Carlos making excuses for Logan.

'Mrs Derby, aren't you being a little—foolish?'

'*Foolish*?' She stared at him incredulously. 'What do you mean?'

Carlos sighed. 'It's not easy for me, Mrs Derby. You're likely to tell me to mind my own business.'

'Yes, I am.' Charlotte's lips trembled. 'But don't let that stop you.'

He rubbed anxiously at the side of his nose. 'I—well, I know Mr Logan pretty well by now . . .'

'I don't doubt it.'

'. . . and I know how he feels about . . . about Robert.'

'You *know*?' Charlotte was filled with consternation.

'Yes, Mrs Derby.'

'But—did Logan tell you?'

Carlos nodded. 'But——' He held up a hand as she would have protested, 'I already had my suspicions.'

Charlotte looped her hair behind her ears with hands that shook. 'I see.' She tried to keep calm. 'How many more people know, I wonder!'

Carlos expelled his breath noisily. 'No one else,' he insisted quietly. 'Remember, I've known Logan Kennedy a long time. You can't live with somebody for a number of years without noticing certain things about them. And Robert—he has a lot of his father's characteristics.'

Charlotte shivered, in spite of her burning limbs. 'And—and will you tell him?'

Carlos shook his head. 'It's not my place, Mrs Derby. And I don't think Mr Logan will tell him either, not unless you want him to.'

Charlotte's head was throbbing. Across the water, she

149

could see Logan and Manoel lowering the dinghy into the water. In a few minutes they would be back again. She turned once more to Carlos.

'Tell me,' she said urgently, 'did Logan know about Robert before we came here?'

Carlos straightened to stand looking out across the water. 'Yes, he knew.'

'But not that—that Robert was his son?'

'No.'

'What—what do you think he will do?'

'Now?' She nodded, and he shrugged his broad shoulders. 'I know what he wants to do.'

'Do you?' she looked up at him nervously, the shaking in no way dispersed. 'What?'

'Don't you know?' Carlos looked back at her. 'He cares for that boy, ma'am. Never doubt that.'

Charlotte got awkwardly to her feet, feeling if anything worse than before. 'And you think Robert should be told, don't you?'

'I think you know he should.'

'But why? Why? Logan's never cared about him all these years.'

'He didn't know, did he?' Carlos was laconic.

Charlotte dug her toes into the sand. 'He didn't care to find out!'

'How could he?' Carlos showed mild impatience. 'You were married to—to someone else, weren't you?'

'Logan left me. He went back to Rio——'

'Yes,' Carlos nodded. 'And he regrets it bitterly. I can tell you that.'

'And is it enough?' she cried, aware of the dinghy nearing the shore. 'Am I expected to forgive him? Just like that?'

'He's forgiven you,' Carlos replied enigmatically, and walked to meet Logan, leaving her wondering exactly what he meant by that.

The dinghy was beached, and Logan came striding up the sandy slope towards her. But rather than risk his touching her again, she went to meet him, brushing aside his concern and walking straight to the dinghy. It was the kind of craft she had seen children using on boating lakes back home. Bigger than average, it took the three of them without capsizing, and Logan and Carlos took an oar each to paddle back to the ketch.

Robert helped her aboard, his face taut with anxiety. 'I'm sorry, Mum,' he began at once, eager to make his explanations before she had a chance to reprove him, 'I never thought you'd go looking for me.' Then: 'Gosh, what have you done to your head?'

'Leave your mother alone, Robert,' Logan told him shortly, as Charlotte subsided with some relief on to the cushions Manoel had placed for her. 'Make yourself useful; get her a glass of fruit juice.'

'Okay.'

Robert grimaced apologetically, and went to do as he was told, much to his mother's surprise. Meanwhile, Logan was rummaging about in one of the underseat lockers, and presently brought out a small medicine box. Charlotte, tense and defensively prepared to do battle with him again, was astonished when he called Elaine over to him, and handed her a couple of tubes indicating clearly what he wanted her to do.

When the Brazilian girl approached her, however, Charlotte held out her hand, and said: 'Thank you, I can do it myself.'

Elaine adopted an obstinate pose. 'Logan asked me to take care of you,' she retorted. 'Please push back your hair so that I can put some of this antiseptic ointment on your forehead.'

Charlotte stared bitterly at Logan, but he was not looking at her. He and Carlos were hauling in the anchor and hoisting the sails, and she was forced to submit to Elaine's ministrations. She felt raw and exposed, both physically and mentally, and so far as she was concerned the whole day had been a disaster.

The swelling dealt with, Elaine turned her attention to

151

the angry-looking burns on Charlotte's arms and legs, and the exposed skin of her midriff.

'You are a fool, Mrs Derby,' she remarked, under cover of the shouted commands Logan was issuing from the helm.

Charlotte refused to be antagonised. 'I know,' she acknowledged quietly. 'I'm not used to such a hot sun.'

'That is not what I meant,' remarked Elaine scornfully. 'Of course, you have been stupid lying in the sun, and what else can you expect from a skin as fair as yours? But I was talking about your—association with Logan.'

Charlotte stiffened. 'There is no association with Logan.'

'No?' Elaine looked sceptical. 'That was not my impression.' She paused. 'What was your relationship with him in London? Were you his mistress?'

'No!' Charlotte was horrified.

'No? But you did sleep with him, did you not, Mrs Derby? Or how else could he have fathered your child, que?'

Charlotte pushed the Brazilian girl's hands away. 'What are you talking about?'

'You forget, *senhora*, I heard what Logan was saying to you in the *caverna*. I am not mistaken. You would not look at me like that, unless you were afraid.'

'*Afraid?*'

'*Sim, senhora.*' Elaine glanced round to assure herself they could not be overheard. 'The boy does not know—of this I am certain. You have not told him because you know that he is already attracted to Logan, and if he learned that Logan was his father ...' She lifted her shoulders expressively.

Charlotte swallowed convulsively. 'If what you say is true, why shouldn't I tell him? I—Logan wants me to.'

Elaine's dark eyebrows ascended. 'I wonder why.'

'What do you mean?'

'Like I said, Mrs Derby, you are a fool. If Logan wants you to tell Robbie, it can be for only one reason. He wants to adopt the boy himself.' She paused. 'You know, do you not, that he intends to marry me?'

'No!' Charlotte's stomach plunged. 'I don't believe it.'

'Why not?' Elaine's lips twisted. 'Because he made love to you?' She shook her head. 'I do not deny that he seems to find you—attractive, and as the mother of his son ...' She sighed. 'But Logan is not a fool. He knows the score. Papa is no philanthropist, Mrs Derby, he is a speculator. And right now, he is speculating on my future.'

'With Logan?'

'With Logan.'

Charlotte was sickened. 'But you can't want to marry a man who—who makes love to other women!'

Elaine shrugged. 'Why not? He makes love to me, too.' She smiled a slow, reminiscent smile which robbed Charlotte of her last shreds of hope. 'He is very good at it, you must agree.'

'Please!' Charlotte couldn't take any more. 'Please—go away!'

'But the cream——'

'Give it to me!' Charlotte almost snatched the tube out of her hand, daubing it liberally over her thighs. 'I can manage. Leave me alone!'

Robert appeared with a glass of iced orange juice. 'I didn't like to interrupt while you were talking to Miss Mendoza——' he began, but Charlotte made a dismissing gesture with her head, taking the juice and drinking thirstily. Robert squatted on the deck at her feet. 'I really am sorry, Mum,' he started again.

'It doesn't matter.' Charlotte was abrupt, but she couldn't help it.

'I had a super time,' Robert went on.

'Good.'

Robert seemed not to notice her monosyllabic replies. 'I found some turtle's eggs,' he went on eagerly. 'Would you like to see them?' He laughed. 'Carlos says that some West Indians think eating turtle's eggs makes you more sexy, or something like that. Anyway, I only took one or two, and

153

Carlos says a turtle can lay more than three hundred eggs at a time.'

'All right, Robert.'

'Would you like to see them?'

'Not right now.'

'No?' Robert looked disappointed for a moment, and then Carlos beckoned to him, and he scrambled to his feet with alacrity, the rueful grin he cast back at her a plea for her understanding.

But after he had gone, she didn't know which was worse—Robert's innocent chatter or the turmoil of the thoughts that plagued her now she was alone. Nothing was the same any more. It was one thing making a decision without anyone else being involved, but suddenly other people were involved, and it was terrifying to think how many people already knew her son's parentage. Had Lisette Fabergé guessed that Logan was Robert's father? Somehow she didn't think so. Lisette was not that kind of person to keep a thing like that to herself.

Which didn't alter the situation at all. She was still left with the disruptingly-growing conviction that if she didn't tell Robert the truth, and he ever found out for himself, he might never forgive her.

Manoel came to ask how she was feeling, but she had no heart to speak to him now. He went away again, probably offended by her offhandedness, but quite honestly, she dreaded him revealing that he, too, had guessed the truth.

Logan approached her some time later, and stood looking down at her with brooding malevolence. 'Do you feel up to talking now?' he inquired curtly, and she closed her eyes against his disturbing sexuality.

'What about?' she countered wearily. 'What is there to say?'

What is there to say?' He repeated her words indistinctly. '*Deus*, Charlotte, there are times when I could——' He broke off, controlling himself with evident difficulty. He dropped down on to the bench seat beside her, legs apart, arms resting along his thighs, his hands hanging between.

'What happened in the cave,' he said, through clenched teeth, 'I think that deserves some consideration, don't you?'

Charlotte half turned away from him. 'You don't have to apologise——'

'My God, I'm not apologising!' he snapped, his voice rising, and falling again as he realised he could be overheard. 'Charlotte, I—I think we should get married.'

'*What?*'

He had her whole attention now. She stared at him disbelievingly, her heart palpitating with the excitement his words had engendered. Was it true? Was he actually asking her to marry him? Had everything Elaine told her been nothing but a pack of lies?

His eyes bored into hers. 'You must have expected it,' he said flatly. 'I don't expect you to make a decision right away. Take as long as you like to think about it. But it seems to be the solution, doesn't it?'

'The ... solution?' His words were having a different effect now. 'What do you mean?'

He raked back his chair wth a careless hand. 'Look, Charlotte, we've got to give this time——'

'What—time?'

'Our relationship. Robert's relationship. I realise that liking someone and finding out that they're your father are two entirely different things——'

'You're doing ... this ... for Robert?'

He swore angrily. 'You're deliberately misunderstanding me.'

'On the contrary, I think I understand you very well.'

'I doubt it However, we'll have the rest of our lives——'

'*No!*' Her lips trembled and she bit on them. 'No.'

'What do you mean—no?'

'What does anyone usually mean? I mean I refuse. The answer's in the negative. I won't do it. Is that clear enough for you?'

'You can't do this to me, Charlotte.' Logan got to his feet as if he could not sit still under her censure. 'I won't accept what you're saying!'

She stared up at him woodenly, praying that he would not notice how her knees were shaking. 'What will you do?' she challenged.

His eyes darkened with anger, and he took a deep breath. 'If you're expecting threats from me, Charlotte, you're going to be disappointed. I won't salve your conscience for you. Robert will never learn anything from me!' And with these words he left, striding over to the wheel to stand stiffly beside Carlos.

Charlotte wanted to cry. Nothing less than tears could soothe the aching void inside her. So, she thought bitterly, Logan was prepared to give up his freedom for the sake of his son, prepared to marry her now when twelve years ago he had abandoned her without compunction. Could Robert possibly mean more to him than his commitment to Elaine? Was he willing to jeopardise his future with the Mendoza Institute by marrying her, when he must know how vindictive Elaine could be? And if so, had she the right to withhold the choice from the one person most intimately involved?

CHAPTER ELEVEN

THE next morning, Charlotte had the greatest difficulty in just getting out of bed. Her legs and arms were raw and painful, and the throbbing in her head was centred around the spreading bruise on her forehead. In addition to which she felt strangely shivery, and guessed she was suffering the after-effects of too much sun. She was glad Carlos left before she was up. He would know immediately what was wrong with her and probably tell Logan, too; that, she could do without.

Trying not to scratch herself, she managed to take a shower and towel herself dry, putting on one of the loose dresses she favoured. Its sleeveless, low-necked style revealed more of her flesh than she liked, but as she couldn't bear anything weighty against her skin, it had to do.

Robert, however, was more perceptive than she had given him credit for being. 'Are you feeling all right, Mum?' he exclaimed, when she came into the kitchen where he already had the kettle boiling. 'You're awfully burned, aren't you? Doesn't it hurt?'

Charlotte managed not to be irritable with him. 'Of course it hurts,' she answered evenly. 'I hope you've taken notice of what reckless sunbathing can do.'

Robert hunched his shoulders, lean and angular in his shorts and tee-shirt. 'My skin doesn't seem to burn like yours,' he remarked, half apologetically Then: 'Mum, don't you think you ought to tell Philippe's mother that you're not going up there today?'

'No, I don't.' An edge had entered Charlotte's voice now. 'Besides, Madame Fabergé may want to join—Mr Kennedy and his guests for lunch today, and someone has to look after Isabelle.'

Robert shrugged. 'She was over at their place last night.

157

I shouldn't think she'll be invited back again today.'

'Oh!'

Charlotte was briefly speechless. She had not known this. As soon as the ketch had moored at the landing, she had excused herself on the pretext of getting out of the sun, and no one had made any attempt to detain her.

At the bungalow she had succeeded in suppressing the storm of weeping which came later until after Robert and Carlos had gone to bed, and if she had thought about Logan at all, it had not been in terms of his entertaining his guests at a dinner party as if nothing untoward had happened.

Now Robert shifted restlessly, hands in the pockets of his shorts. 'I've had my breakfast, Mum. Is it all right if I go?'

Charlotte turned off the kettle. 'Go? Go where?'

Robert coloured. 'Carlos said I might help him this morning. The station wagon's developed an oil leak, and he's going to show me how to change a gasket.'

Charlotte sank down weakly into a chair, absurdly near to tears again. 'Do what you like,' she said, without expression.

Robert hesitated. 'I really do think you ought to take the day off, Mum,' he mumbled. 'Go back to bed...'

Charlotte managed to school her features into a smile. 'Don't be silly.' She gestured towards the door. 'Go along. Go and do your mechanicking. See you later.'

With evidently mixed feelings, Robert left her, and wearily she got to her feet again and made some tea. The hot liquid was soothing, but it would take more than tea to restore her, she thought despairingly. Pushing her cup aside she rested her elbows on the table, supporting her head on her hands, feeling a total sense of dejection.

She had been sitting like that for some time when a sound made her lift her head, and she stared in dismay at the denim-clad legs on a level with her vision. Her eyes travelled up over masculine thighs to the leather belt slung round his hips, and from there over the muscled expanse of his chest revealed by the denim waistcoat hanging open

158

from his shoulders. She didn't need to look into the lean dark face or see the black hair clinging wetly to his neck to know who was standing there, watching her.

'Wh-what do you want now?' she asked, unable to hide the tremor in her voice, and he uttered an angry imprecation as he came to stand before the table.

'Can't you guess?' he demanded. 'Your—*our* son was concerned about you.'

She drew an unsteady breath. 'There—there was no need——'

'Damn you, I'll decide when there's a need!' he muttered. 'Exactly what do you think you are going to do today?'

She gasped. 'What I usually do.'

'No!'

She pushed back her chair and got to her feet. 'I don't intend to argue with you, Logan.'

'Oh, don't you?' His tone was sardonic. He came round the table towards her. 'That is good news.'

'Logan——'

'I suggest you go back to bed. I want Stevens to take a look at you.'

'I won't!' Charlotte quivered. 'I—I meant I'm perfectly all right. And Lisette is expecting me——'

'To hell with Lisette!' Logan's hot breath fanned her forehead. 'Charlotte, I don't want to hurt you but, God help me, if you don't do as I say, I'm going to have to.'

'Oh, Logan, please!' She wrung her hands, looking up at him unwillingly, realising that fighting him simply would not do any good. 'Why can't you leave me alone? I don't torment you. Why do you persist in persecuting me?'

'You don't torment me?' His dry smile was without humour. 'Charlotte, you can have no idea what you do to me!' His hands lifted almost against his will to cradle her face. 'What do I have to do to make you listen to me?'

Charlotte tried to move her head from side to side. 'Why did you bring me here?' she cried bitterly.

His hands fell to his sides. 'Why do you think?'

She shrugged. 'To make me suffer?'

His lips thinned. 'And if I did?' He shook his head. 'I don't know. I had to know——' He broke off abruptly. 'Tell me something—why didn't you let me know that you were expecting a child? Didn't I have the right to be told?'

Charlotte put a shaking hand to her head. 'Oh, Logan, it's too early in the morning——'

'*Deus!*' he interrupted her violently. 'When is it not too early—or too late—or the wrong time, or we'll be overheard —or you don't want to talk about it? God, Charlotte, I've been more than patient! You heedlessly deny me knowledge of the first eleven years of my son's life, and then calmly propose to separate us again without even telling me why?' The knuckles of his clenched fists showed white through the brown skin. 'All right, I have to accept that you don't regret what you've done, but don't you think you owe me an explanation?'

There seemed to be something wrong with Charlotte's vision. Every now and then Logan's profile swam into two, and she found it almost impossible to distinguish which was the man and which was the reflection.

'You—you went back to Rio,' she stammered. 'You—you weren't there when I found out.'

'Goddammit, there are such things as telegrams—telephones; the university could have told you where I was!'

Charlotte made a negative gesture. 'You—you think I would have done that?' she demanded unsteadily.

'Obviously you didn't.'

'I have some pride left, Logan.'

'Pride? *Pride?* What has pride got to do with it?' He raked long fingers through his hair. 'Did you imagine that because I didn't know about it, the child was any less mine?'

'You didn't care!' she protested.

'I didn't *know!*' he retorted coldly. 'Charlotte, Matthew knew where I was. He had my address.'

She stared at him disbelievingly, swaying a little. 'He didn't!'

160

'He *did*!' he insisted inexorably. 'But perhaps you didn't tell him about the baby until afterwards, hmm?' Contempt twisted his features. 'Why didn't I think of that before? Perhaps the poor sod thought the child was his. My God, what a rude awakening he must have had! No wonder he cut you off without a penny——'

'It's not true!' She could not allow him to believe that. 'Matthew did know. He *did*!'

Logan was staring at her through narrowed eyes. 'Can you prove that?'

She trembled. 'Can you prove he didn't?'

Logan uttered an oath. 'Charlotte, I——'

But what he was about to say she did not hear. The dizziness she had been fighting ever since she got to her feet was overwhelming her, and for the first time in her life, she lost consciousness.

She didn't remember much of what happened for the rest of that day. She opened her eyes to a darkened room, and later Michael Stevens came to see her, calm and competent, despite his shorts and sweat shirt.

'Sunstroke,' he diagnosed mildly. 'Not too severe a case, but enough to keep you here for the next couple of days.'

'But Lisette——' she began weakly, and he put a reproving finger on her lips.

'Rest,' he told her firmly. 'Now, I'm just going to give you something to ease the pain ...'

She fell asleep soon afterwards, and in the fleeting moments of consciousness she had throughout that day and the night that followed, she guessed he had sedated her. Not that she cared. At least in oblivion she was free from the problems which would beset her as soon as she was fit again, not least the uncertainty which Logan's words had aroused. Had Matthew really known Logan's address all along? Could he have kept it from her knowing that she might feel obliged to at least inform Logan of her condition? It was unacceptable, and besides, thinking made her

161

headache worse. She allowed herself to drift, and when next she surfaced it was daylight.

To her surprise, Lisette was sitting by her bed, and she seemed relieved when Charlotte opened her eyes.

'Hi!'

'Hi!' Charlotte's lips were dry, and her throat felt parched.

'How are you?' Lisette sounded genuinely concerned, and Charlotte managed a cracked smile.

'I'll live.'

She licked her lips, and immediately Lisette got up and indicated the jug of iced fruit juice on the table beside the bed. 'Would you like a drink?'

Charlotte nodded. 'Please.'

Lisette poured some into a glass and coming to the bed, helped her up, holding the glass to her lips.

'I'm not an invalid,' said Charlotte, at last, sinking back on to the pillows. 'You should be berating me. I caused this to happen. I'm to blame.'

'Oh, forget it.' Lisette glanced carelessly about the room. 'Say, would you mind if I had a cigarette? I'm gasping for one.'

Charlotte had to smile. 'No, go ahead.'

'Well, so long as *Nurse* Stevens doesn't come back and catch me at it!' remarked Lisette dryly, lighting up. 'Cigarettes in the sickroom and all that.' She raised her eyes heavenward. 'Seriously, though, are you sure you're feeling better?'

'Yes, of course.' Charlotte could feel that her limbs were no longer burning. 'What time is it?'

'Almost noon. Helen had to go and see to the children's lunch, so I said I'd stay.'

'Helen? Helen's been here?'

'All night. Someone had to stay with you, and Mike didn't think Carlos was entirely suitable.' She grimaced wryly.

'Carlos?' Charlotte could feel the creeping agony of recollection enveloping her. 'I—where's Robert?'

162

'With Helen,' replied Lisette indifferently. 'Along with Philippe and Isabelle. She's a regular little mother, isn't she? But then you know that.'

Charlotte's lips formed Logan's name, but the word remained unspoken. However, Lisette must have perceived her thoughts, and said lightly: 'Logan's not here. He left early this morning with the Mendozas. They've flown back to St Thomas.'

'Oh!' An anguished sound was stifled in her throat. 'I—do you know when he's coming back?'

Lisette shook her head. 'No.' Then she leant forward, her eyes perceptibly brighter. 'I'm leaving, too.'

Charlotte struggled up on to her elbows, ignoring the pain that seared through her head. 'You are?'

'Yes.' Lisette nodded. 'Isn't it exciting? I'm going home, back to London. Senhor Mendoza's arranging it.'

'Senhor Mendoza?' Charlotte couldn't take it in.

'Yes.' Lisette explained patiently: 'Pierre was employed by the Mendoza Institute, too. When he died, there was some talk about compensation, but it never came to anything. Anyway, it turns out that Logan's been working behind the scenes, so to speak, and he's got Mendoza to agree to a lump sum. Twenty thousand pounds! What do you think about that?'

Charlotte slumped back on to the pillows. 'I—that's great, Lisette,' she managed; and it was, for Lisette.

'I know. I can hardly believe it.'

Charlotte refused to consider the consequences as far as she was concerned. After all, she had made up her mind to leave long ago. 'Wh-what will you do?' she asked.

'Well, get a flat, for a start. And a nanny for the kids.' She coloured at the implication. 'Oh, I'm sorry, Mrs Derby. But I don't mean you. I want someone who can live in, someone younger. Someone I can boss about. Someone I don't feel inferior to.'

Charlotte would have protested, but Lisette went on: 'It's true. You are different from me—I know that. Logan knows it, too.' She paused. 'Anyway, after that—getting the flat, I

163

mean—I'm going to get a job. I don't have to, really, although the capital won't last for ever. But I want to. I like going out—meeting different people. Different men!' Her eyes sparkled. 'I might even go back to the university. I was a damn good typist.'

'I'm sure you were.'

Charlotte lay back on the pillows, wondering how long it would take for her to recover her strength. If only it were possible to get away from here before Logan returned. Robert would be disappointed, but he would get over it. Except ... Except that until Logan came back and paid her her salary, she couldn't afford their return tickets ...

Thinking about Robert brought back all her doubts about Matthew, and she knew she wouldn't rest until she had discovered for herself whether Logan had been telling the truth. If Matthew had known his address, perhaps she had done Logan a terrible injustice, although nothing could alter the fact that he had gone away without bothering to find out for himself whether she had been all right.

Nevertheless, Lisette's words had given her an idea. Maybe someone at the university would know whether Matthew had known Logan's home address. The principal had been a friend of his, although she realised that he might well have retired by now. Even so, it was worth a try, and something to give her a reason to get well.

Robert arrived with Helen a little while later. The doctor's wife had prepared her a delicious vegetable broth, and Charlotte found she was quite hungry. Robert sat with her while she ate, and it was obvious from his conversation that he had been told not to bother her with anything.

Eventually Charlotte put the remains of the broth aside, and said quietly: 'What would you say if I told you we were leaving here?'

The consternation in his face was swiftly masked. 'Leaving?'

'Yes. You knew we would be, sooner or later,' she added, pleating the bedcover. 'Have you heard that the Fabergés are going back to London?'

'We're going with them?' exclaimed Robert in surprise, but his mother shook her head.

'No. We're going on our own.'

'Back to London?' Robert hunched his shoulders.

'That's right.' She tried to make light of it. 'It's summer in England, and we'll have all the school holidays to make our plans; fix you up with a school and me with a job.'

Robert got up from his seat and paced heavily about the room, hands in pockets, his thin face mirroring his disappointment. 'Must we?' he demanded at last, stopping to confront her.

Charlotte's heart thumped. 'You know we do.'

Robert sniffed. 'Why? Why can't we stay on here? Couldn't you look after Mrs Stevens's children like you used to look after Madame Fabergé's?'

'No.' Charlotte could feel a trickle of perspiration sliding down her spine. 'Robert, Mrs Stevens is perfectly capable of looking after her own children.'

'Well—well, what about Mr Kennedy?'

The room was shaded, and Charlotte was glad of it. 'Wh-what about Mr Kennedy?'

'I don't know. Couldn't you be—housekeeper to him or something? Carlos could do with some help——'

'No, Robert.'

'Why not?' Robert looked sulky. 'I like it here.'

'I know you do. But you've had a lovely holiday——'

'Huh!'

'—and now it's time to go back to work.'

'I don't want to go back to work.'

Charlotte's patience snapped. 'Oh, for heaven's sake, Robert! Stop being so selfish! How do you think I feel when you talk like this? I've got the responsibility to plan for our futures, not you, and if I say we're going back to London, we're going back to London!'

Surprisingly, her words did not arouse their usual reaction. 'When?' he asked sullenly.

'When what?'

'When are we going back to London?'

'I don't know. Soon.'

'After Mr Kennedy gets back?'

'Perhaps.' Charlotte was deliberately evasive.

'Perhaps?' Robert looked dismayed. 'What do you mean?'

'I mean, I don't know. Why? What does it matter?' Charlotte pushed back the weight of her hair with a trembling hand.

'He said he'd see me when he got back!' exclaimed Robert distractedly.

'Well, he might not. What of it?'

Robert's lips pursed. 'I don't see why we have to go back. Why can't I have any say in the matter?'

'I'm your mother, Robert.'

'I know it.' Robert sniffed again. 'I just wish I had a father!' And with these words he charged out of the room.

After he had gone, Charlotte felt limp. Dear God, she thought weakly, children could say the cruellest things! Of course, he couldn't understand, but even so ...

She felt stronger the next day, and the headache had almost completely disappeared. Against Michael Stevens's advice, she got up in the afternoon and put her clothes on. She needed to feel she was getting better, and lying in bed would not hasten the cure.

She had seen next to nothing of Robert since the previous afternoon, and his absence began to play on her nerves like an aching tooth. She learned two days later that he was spending most of his time with Carlos, but that did nothing to reassure her. On the contrary, she had the feeling that she and her son were on opposite sides of a wall which was getting higher by the hour. It was useless telling herself now that she should have stuck to her guns in the first place and kept him away from Logan. It would have been an impossible task. And besides, nothing could alter the fact that Logan was his father and therefore had as much legal right to his company as she had.

With a feeling of futility, she began to pack her belongings, deliberately leaving Robert's things until last, curiously

166

loath to take the step which would alienate them from his father once and for all.

Helen came upon her as she was rinsing out some nylon undies and exclaimed at once: 'What do you think you're doing, Charlotte? You're supposed to be resting this week.'

Charlotte gave her an apologetic grimace. 'I needed the occupation.'

'Why? What's wrong? Are you sorry the Fabergés are leaving?'

Charlotte shook her head. 'Oh, no. No, nothing like that.' She forced a smile. 'Just—depression, I think.'

Helen sighed. 'It's to do with Logan, isn't it?' She hesitated as Charlotte pretended to be concentrating on a thread of lace. 'What's happened? Has he told you he's going to marry Elaine?'

'No!' But Charlotte couldn't hide the pain in her eyes. Then, distractedly: 'Is he?'

Helen shrugged uncomfortably. 'So her father says. We were invited to the beach house for drinks one evening— you know, the evening before you were taken ill. And according to Mendoza, everything's fixed except the date.'

'Oh!' Charlotte bent her head again. 'I see.'

Helen stared at her unhappily. 'You're in love with him, aren't you?' she asked perceptively. 'I guessed you were. That day you had coffee with me—I knew there was something ...' She paused, but Charlotte said nothing, and presently, she added: 'He's an attractive man, I know. Heavens, even I can see that. But—well, Charlotte, you'll get over it.'

'Will I?' Charlotte dried her hands on a towel, and then looked at her through red-rimmed eyes. 'Can you guarantee it?'

Helen felt dreadful. 'Oh, love! I'm sorry. I shouldn't have mentioned it. Me and my big mouth!'

'It's all right, really.' Charlotte sank down into a chair, suddenly weary. 'I know it's got to be faced.'

Helen took the chair opposite. 'That's right. That's the

167

way to take it. Lord, you've only known the man a month! You'll soon forget him.'

'No, I won't.' Charlotte sounded curiously defeated. She looked across at Helen's confused face and then said flatly: 'You might as well know—Logan is Robert's father.'

Helen could not have looked more shocked. 'Logan—is Robert's father?' she echoed.

'That's right.' Charlotte sighed. 'Now do you understand my problem?'

'Does Robert know?'

'No.'

'And Logan?'

'Oh, yes. Yes.'

Helen shook her head. 'And?'

'He—he asked me to marry him.'

Helen's expression was ludicrous. 'He what?' She gave a little shake of her head as if to clear her brain. 'Charlotte, are you telling me you turned him down? When? When you were first pregnant—or recently?'

'A few days ago,' replied Charlotte quietly.

'But why? You just——'

'He wants his son, Helen, that's all. I won't marry him for that.'

Helen leaned back in her chair. 'But you love the man!'

Charlotte lifted her shoulders. 'What kind of marriage would that be? He doesn't need my permission to take Robert from me.' She bent her head as tears threatened. 'I'm not so sure he's not done it already.'

'Why?'

'Robert. He doesn't want us to leave.'

'And you do?'

'I have to,' said Charlotte bitterly. 'I just wish we could leave before Logan gets back.'

'Why can't you?' Helen frowned.

Charlotte shifted awkwardly. 'I—my fare was paid out here but not back. And as I haven't received any salary yet ...'

'I see.' Helen nodded understandingly. 'But once you've been paid . . .'

'Oh, yes. Once Logan gets back and pays me,' agreed Charlotte miserably. Then she tried to pull herself together. 'I'm sorry, Helen—involving you in all this. But I had to tell somebody.'

Helen stretched out her hand and patted her soothingly on the shoulder. 'Don't be silly. I just wish there was some way——' She broke off abruptly. 'Of course! Why didn't I think of it before? I could lend you the money——'

'Oh, no!' Charlotte looked horrified.

'Why not?' Helen was eager now. 'Why shouldn't I? You can send me a cheque when you're in funds again. Heavens . . .' She spread an expressive hand. 'What do I need money here for? There's nothing to spend it on. I'd like to help you, Charlotte, really.'

Charlotte drew a trembling breath. It was a temptation. But could she take Robert away from here without giving him one last chance to see his father? She doubted she could. She doubted he would go.

'Thank you, Helen,' she said at last, 'but I can't do it. It's running away, and I've already run too far.'

Helen sighed. 'Well . . . You know best, I suppose.'

Charlotte bent her head. 'I don't know whether I do, but—thanks anyway.'

Helen dismissed her gratitude with a regretful smile. Then she said firmly: 'If you should change your mind, you know. The offer is still open.'

It had done her good talking to Helen, and Charlotte prepared the evening meal with more enthusiasm than of late. It was good to know she had an escape route if she needed it, and somehow once the door was open, her position seemed less fraught.

Robert appeared as she was making the dressing for the salad. He looked into the kitchen, but went straight to his room, and didn't come out again until she called him.

'Have you had a good day?' she asked brightly, determined to ignore the long face he was wearing.

Robert shrugged offhandedly, and helped himself to a roll. 'It was all right.'

'Have you been snorkelling?' Charlotte persisted, but he mimed that his mouth was full and couldn't answer her. When he had emptied his mouth, however, he quickly filled it again, and she refused to pander to his vanity by appealing to him.

When the meal was over, he would have left the room again, but tonight Charlotte determined that he should wash the dishes, and his response to her request was to bang all the plates together in the sink so that one smashed and splintered, cutting his finger.

Charlotte was out of her chair in a minute, running his hand beneath the cold tap, removing the broken piece of plate to the waste bin. Then, still without speaking, she got the tin of Bandaid plaster from her suitcase, and secured one round the injury.

'Thanks, Mum.' Robert was subdued now, and judging from his expression near to tears, but Charlotte refused to feel sympathy for him.

'You'll survive!' she remarked dryly, and indicated the rest of the dishes. 'Try not to break any more. Mr—er—Kennedy might not be too happy about us smashing up the place before we leave.'

His chin jutting, Robert dipped his hands into the soapy water and began washing the other plates. 'We are leaving, then,' he muttered in an undertone, so that she could hardly hear him.

Charlotte sighed. 'You know we are.'

'When?'

'In a day or two.'

Robert glanced round at her. 'Carlos says that Mr Kennedy will be angry if we leave without seeing him.'

'Oh, does he?' Charlotte stilled the trembling that threatened to start once more. 'Well, what Carlos says doesn't concern me.'

Robert looked mutinous. 'I thought what Mr Kennedy said did.'

'Is that supposed to mean something?'

He moved his shoulders indifferently. 'You seemed to like him well enough on the boat.'

'Did I?'

'Yes.' Robert was defensive. 'When everybody else was sleeping, you let him——' He flushed. 'Well, anyway, it's not fair.'

'What's not fair?'

'You—making us leave here!' Robert turned fully round now. 'You know Mr Kennedy doesn't want us to go, but you won't listen to him!'

'What are you talking about?' Charlotte stared at him in real confusion. 'What do you know about it?'

Robert bent his head, shifting his weight from one foot to the other, obviously discomfited by her questions. 'You *know*!' he muttered sullenly.

Charlotte felt a cold hand touch her stomach. Like Logan and Carlos, and Elaine, too—did Robert know his father's identity? Her mind flipped back alarmingly over her conversation with Logan on the yacht. Could Robert have heard something? Was this behaviour the result of resentment at knowledge withheld? But no! At that time, she had not known that Logan suspected the truth, and nothing had been said to enlighten the boy. And yet...

'I think you'd better tell me exactly what you mean, Robert,' she said now, amazed at how calm she sounded, when inside her stomach was churning.

Robert hunched his shoulders, assuming an obstinate stance. 'I heard,' he said, and her fears were rekindled.

'You heard?' Charlotte's voice was strangled. 'Heard what?'

'What Miss Mendoza said,' retorted Robert sulkily, and Charlotte's cheeks paled remembering what Elaine had said.

'I—I see,' she got out at last, wishing she felt stronger. 'So—so you know——'

'—that Mr Kennedy wants to adopt me, yes,' Robert finished, before she could complete the revealing statement she had been about to make. 'I know I wasn't supposed to hear,

171

but I was bringing your orange, and—well, just imagine! A man like that wanting to adopt me! Just like—just like when Matthew Derby took you to live with him.' He made a dismissing gesture. 'Being able to go with him on all his expeditions, living like Carlos does, in all the most exciting places in the world! Wouldn't that be fabulous?'

Charlotte's body sagged. 'You think so,' she managed, faintly, trying to pull herself together again with difficulty. But the trauma of imagining he knew the whole truth and then learning he didn't even know the half of it was debilitating.

'Do I?' Robert said now, his eyes brighter than they had been for days. 'I mean'—he tried to justify himself—'we're interested in the same things, Mr Kennedy and me. I think I'd like to be a biologist when I grow up. And with him for a father ...'

Charlotte turned her back on him, making her way to the door with a feeling of unreality muzzing the edges of her mind. It was like a bad dream, but unlike a bad dream it would not be banished by pinching herself. It seemed as if everything was conspiring against her, and no amount of wishing could make it better.

In her room, she stared about her blankly, not entirely capable of assimilating what she had planned to do. But one thing seemed painfully obvious. She could not take Robert away from here without telling him the truth, and right now that was beyond her capabilities.

She sank down on to the side of the bed, burying her face in her hands. She had never felt so lost and alone, not even when she had first discovered she was pregnant. At least then she had had Matthew, although now even his sympathy seemed suspect.

She was so lost in her own misery that she did not hear the door open, and therefore she was startled when Robert dropped to his knees beside her, wrapping his arms around her and pressing his face into her lap.

'I'm sorry, I'm sorry,' he sobbed bitterly, his tears soaking through the thin material of her dress. 'I've been a pig!

172

I'm sorry. I didn't mean to upset you, honestly.'

A little of the pain constricting her heart was eased. With tender fingers, she stroked back the dark hair, so exactly like his father's, and bent her head to speak against his cheek.

'It's all right, darling,' she reassured him gently. 'I was just feeling down, that's all.'

Robert sniffed miserably. 'It's all my fault.'

'No, it's not. Don't be foolish. I haven't been well, you know. People sometimes get very depressed when they've been ill.'

Robert lifted his head doubtfully. 'Are you sure?'

'Of course I'm sure.' Charlotte forced a smile. 'Now stop feeling sorry for yourself, and make me a cup of tea.'

But although she managed to satisfy him that she was not distressed over his behaviour, the problem remained, and as she got ready for bed that night she knew what she was going to do. She had had eleven years of Robert's life. The best eleven years, she liked to think. He was growing up now, and Logan would never know the thrill of seeing him take his first step and speaking his first word. She had had the hugs and kisses, which with both parents she would have had to share, and surely now she could afford to be generous. Robert needed his father more than his mother at this stage of his development, and she could not deprive him of that opportunity for purely selfish reasons. She hadn't told Robert about his father, but Logan would, and maybe in a couple of years they could meet again—as friends. She would take the money Helen offered and go, before Logan returned. Helen would help her. She would understand. And Robert, the child he really was, would soon forget.

CHAPTER TWELVE

LONDON was very warm, the atmosphere heavy after the clean air of Avocado Cay. For several days Charlotte was too exhausted to summon up the energy to do anything, too drained both emotionally and physically to care where she was or what was going on about her.

It had been surprisingly easy to get away from the island. Expecting a hitch at the last moment or, terrifyingly, Logan's sudden reappearance, she found her eventual journey from San Cristobal to Tortola had been something of an anti-climax.

It had been agonising leaving Robert. That last morning, letting him go off to find Carlos with only a casual word of farewell, had torn her to pieces, but she knew if she broke down and told him what she planned to do, he would never let her go alone.

Helen had tried to argue with her. But she had known that she was wasting her time, and had offered no reproaches. Only someone intimately involved could try to persuade her, and while she knew she could never have done such a thing, she had to admire Charlotte's courage. Nevertheless, there had been moments on the quay, before the launch sailed, when Charlotte would have given anything for someone to have told her what she was doing was wrong.

In London, she checked into the cheapest hotel she could find, booking a single room without bath, overlooking a row of equally cheap houses. It was near Shepherds Bush, in an area which had once been prosperous, but which now struggled against becoming a slum.

She slept a lot those first few days, only eating when the pangs of hunger became unbearable. She felt as though she was living in limbo, not really believing her situation, but similarly accepting that she was unable to escape from it. She looked at her reflection in the spotted dressing table mirror only rarely, because she knew she had to find employment, and the sight of her haggard features filled her with despair. Who, she wondered, would be prepared to hire such a gaunt-looking creature?

Of course, there would be all manner of formalities to go into first. She had no National Insurance card, no indication of what she had earned that year, or what income tax she was due to pay. But first, before entering into those complications, she wanted to go to the university and find out whether Dr Mannering had retired. It was a foolish whim in the circumstances, but one which she had promised herself she would obey.

The university was in Kensington, and a week after she had returned to England, Charlotte caught a bus which would take her some way towards her destination. It was the first time she had been out, other than to buy food, and she had the ridiculous sensation that everyone must know and was looking at her. She had put on denim trousers, and a blue cotton shirt, not wanting to draw attention to herself and had left her hair loose to hide the hollows in her pale cheeks.

The receptionist at the inquiry desk regarded her curiously when she asked for Dr Mannering. 'No, he hasn't retired yet, Mrs Derby,' she replied, after Charlotte had vouchsafed her identity, and the doubts she had had. 'But the university's closed at the moment——'

'Oh, I know that,' Charlotte interrupted her quickly. 'But I do want to contact Dr Mannering if I can.'

'Well ...' The girl looked thoughtful. 'As it happens, he is in the building today. Hang on—I'll see if I can reach him.'

'Thank you.'

Charlotte hovered uncertainly about the coolly tiled lobby, waiting while the receptionist made several calls.

175

The panelled walls were hung with dark-framed pictures of solemn-eyed individuals in caps and gowns, and an enormous plaque denoting the year the university was founded. Not the most comforting of surroundings, but she was in no mood to care.

'Mrs Derby?' The receptionist was beckoning, and Charlotte hurried towards her. 'I've managed to contact Dr Mannering, and he says he'll see you, so long as whatever it is you have to say doesn't take up too much of his time.'

'Oh, no, it won't.' Charlotte hugged her bag to her breast. 'Where do I go?'

Dr Mannering awaited her in his office, an imposing room on the first floor. Here again, the walls were panelled, and a framed portrait of the man himself hung behind his desk. He frowned as she came into the room, obviously trying to place her, and then his eyes widened in surprise.

'Of course,' he said politely, holding out his hand, 'you're Matthew Derby's wife—or rather his widow. I'm sorry, that was tactless. Tell me,' as she subsided into the chair he indicated, 'what can I do for you?'

Charlotte didn't know how to begin. 'I—I hoped I'd still find you here, Dr Mannering. I was afraid you might have retired.'

His smile was dry. 'There's life in the old dog yet.'

'Oh, no ...' She coloured. 'That's not what I meant. Ony it seems so long ago since—since Matthew had anything to do with the university.'

'Yes.' Dr Mannering seated himself opposite her, crossing his legs. He was an angular man, tall and inclined to stoop now, but approachable, for all that. 'I'm afraid your late husband and I had different views about—a number of things.'

'Yes.' Charlotte shifted awkwardly. 'I—er—I've been living out of the country for the last month.'

'Since Matthew died?'

'Soon after, yes.'

'I was sorry to hear about his death.' Dr Mannering

176

sounded sincere. 'He was quite a young man.' His eyes flickered over her pale face. 'Was it very bad?'

Realising he must think her appearance had to do with Matthew's death, Charlotte felt worse than ever. 'As a matter of fact, it was over fairly quickly,' she said. 'And—and towards the end, I'm afraid he didn't want to see me.'

'I'm sorry.'

'Yes.' She shrugged. 'But it's over now. We have to get over these things.'

'Of course.' He inclined his head. 'And you have a son, I believe, who must be a great comfort to you at this time.'

Charlotte felt a terrible yawning sense of emptiness opening inside her, and it was all she could do not to moan aloud at the agony it caused her. But somehow she managed to choke back her misery, and say carefully: 'As a matter of fact, Dr Mannering, that is what I wanted to talk to you about.'

He frowned. 'Your son?'

'Yes.'

He leaned forward, resting his arms upon the desk. 'In what way can I help you?'

She swallowed convulsively. This was more difficult than even she had imagined. 'I—well, it's not easy for me to ask you what it is I want to ask you, Dr Mannering,' she faltered, realising how disjointed that sounded.

'No?'

'No.' She twisted the strap of her bag round her fingers. 'Do you—is it possible you remember a student of yours from some years back? A—a Brazilian called Logan——'

'—Kennedy,' supplied Dr Mannering flatly. 'Of course I remember him.'

'You do?' Charlotte was amazed.

Dr Mannering made an impatient gesture. 'It's not every day that one of my students is threatened with an accusation of statutory rape, Mrs Derby,' he remarked coldly. 'Of course I remember him. I myself suggested it might be best if he returned to Rio de Janeiro.'

177

Charlotte was stunned. She had known nothing about this. That Logan should have been involved with another girl whose parents had threatened him with court proceedings was bad enough, but she had left Robert in the charge of such a man!

'I—I didn't know,' she stammered faintly.

Now it was Dr Mannering's turn to look shocked. 'Come, Mrs Derby,' he protested, 'you must have done.'

Charlotte shook her head. 'How—how could I?'

Dr Mannering stared at her. 'Do you mean to say that Matthew didn't tell you?'

'Matthew?' Charlotte put a confused hand to her head. 'What—what has Matthew got to do with it?'

'He made the complaint!' exclaimed Dr Mannering forcefully. 'My God, do you mean it wasn't true?'

Charlotte thought she was going to faint. It was strange, because she wasn't a fainting person, but just lately she seemed to have very little stamina. She must have looked ill, because Dr Mannering got up from his chair and came round the desk towards her, quickly opening a decanter on a side table and offering her some strong-smelling spirit. It was brandy, and she sipped it obediently, unwilling to collapse here and possibly let him see where she was staying.

'Are you feeling better?' he asked at last, and she managed to nod her head, putting down the glass and making an effort to appear calm. He resumed his seat behind the desk, and then, folding his hands together, he said: 'Exactly what was your relationship with young Kennedy, Mrs Derby?'

Charlotte hesitated. But she had started this and she had to go on. As briefly as possible she outlined how she met Logan, their attraction for one another, and less coolly its ultimate outcome.

'I—I should tell you that—that Matthew and I had—had had a row,' she murmured, hectic colour giving her cheeks a feverish appearance. 'When—when I went to Logan's hotel room, I—I was as much to blame for what happened as he was.'

Dr Mannering pushed back his chair with an impatient gesture. 'Do you mean to tell me that my call to Kennedy came in while you were still there?'

Charlotte remembered the telephone call from the principal only too well. 'I—I suppose it must have done. Unless you rang a second time . . .'

'There was no second call, Mrs Derby.' Dr Mannering paced to the windows, hands clasped tightly behind his back. 'Your—that is to say, Derby rang me and told me Kennedy had seduced his ward. He made it very clear what his intentions would be if one of my students persisted in pursuing such a course.'

Charlotte was horrified, hardly able to comprehend what this could mean to herself—and to Logan. 'You—you mean, Matthew rang you after I had left the house?'

'I suppose he must have done.' Dr Mannering turned back to face her. 'You're saying you knew none of this?'

'No. *No!*' Charlotte was distracted. 'Please . . .' She gazed at him imploringly. 'If there's anything else you think I should know . . .'

He came back to the desk, regarding her gravely. 'Why has all this come up now?' he asked. 'Surely the past is dead and gone.'

'Oh, no.' Charlotte shook her head vigorously. 'I'm afraid I haven't told you the whole story. I—my son—the son you mentioned earlier. Logan was the boy's father.'

'You mean—you passed him off——'

'No. No, that's not what I mean.' Charlotte spoke frantically. 'Matthew knew. He knew he couldn't have any children—he was injured, during the war. He didn't like to talk about it, but it's true. His brother can verify that. That—that's why Robert and I left the country. He left us nothing.'

'My dear Mrs Derby——'

179

'Oh, please! Won't you go on? If there is anything else I should know ...'

'Where does Kennedy come into all this?' The principal was determined to have all the facts. 'Does he know about the boy?'

'He does now.' Charlotte sighed. 'Oh—I don't know why, he must have kept me under observation over the years, and when he knew Matthew was dead, he was instrumental in getting me a job as nursemaid to the children of a friend of his. That was when—when he learned about Robert.'

'I see.' Dr Mannering nodded, subsiding into his seat again. 'Well, let me see—what more can I tell you that you don't already know?' He frowned. 'The whole affair was very upsetting, you know. Kennedy was an intelligent man, a fine student. We were sorry he had to leave, but in the circumstances ...' He sighed. 'What I can't understand is why you didn't speak to him yourself afterwards. Surely that would have been the fairest thing to do.'

Charlotte bent her head. 'He—he left before I could contact him.'

'Before *you* could contact *him*!' Dr Mannering stared at her aghast. 'My dear young lady, I know that young Kennedy tried several times to see you—to speak to you. I believe he wrote several letters, but they were all returned unopened.'

Charlotte had thought she had heard it all, but now she felt utterly shattered. 'You mean—you mean Matthew ...' She couldn't go on, and Dr Mannering, after a moment, nodded.

'It seems as though he must have done,' he exclaimed perplexedly. 'Oh, dear, oh, dear! I had no idea ...'

'Nor did I!' cried Charlotte, getting to her feet to pace restlessly about the room. 'Do you realise what this means? If—if Logan tried to get in touch with me, he didn't just—abandon me.'

'And you thought he did?' Dr Mannering's expression mirrored his distaste at the whole affair. 'But surely you had Kennedy's address?'

'Not in Rio. And—and Matthew rang the university, or so he said, and ascertained that Logan had left the country.'

Dr Mannering spread his hands. 'Well, Matthew certainly had Kennedy's address, had he chosen to give it to you. In the beginning, if you remember, he evinced an intense interest in the young man's work. It was only later——'

'After Logan and I fell in love,' said Charlotte bitterly.

'—that he became opposed to him.' Dr Mannering rose to his feet again. 'If only I'd known ... Although,' he shook his head, 'Matthew was your guardian. The law would have been on his side, one can't deny that.'

Charlotte nodded, too numb now to think straight. 'Well—well, thank you for your time,' she managed unsteadily. 'You—you've answered all my questions. Thank you.'

Dr Mannering took the hand she held out in farewell with more warmth than at their meeting. 'I'm sorry I had to be the bearer of such bad news,' he said regretfully. He paused. 'Console yourself with the thought that Matthew must have loved you very much.'

'Yes.' Charlotte found his words cold comfort. 'Goodbye, then.'

'Goodbye, Mrs Derby.'

Outside, she breathed deeply of the cooler air. It had been warm in Dr Mannering's study with the sun streaming through his windows, and it was easier to think away from his too-knowledgeable eyes.

She slung her bag over her shoulder. So Logan had not deserted her, after all. And she had refused to listen to him, had practically driven him into the arms of another woman! Oh, Matthew, she thought despairingly, you've certainly made me pay for any humiliation you suffered when my mother chose another man!

The path to the gates was tree-lined, and she was walking along with her head down when she almost collided with a man coming from the opposite direction. She lifted

181

her head, an apology spilling automatically from her lips, and then gasped incredulously: '*Logan!*'

And Logan it was, vaguely unfamiliar in a dark lounge suit and grey shirt, his lean features hard and implacable. Before she could formulate any words at all, he had grabbed her upper arms in an iron grip, and with scarcely-leashed anger, exploded: '*Deus!* So I've found you! What in God's name do you think you are doing?'

'Logan.' She said his name again, hardly daring to accept that it was really him. She touched his cheek, but he flinched away from her. 'Logan, oh, Logan—I can't believe it's really you!'

'I'll bet you can't!' he muttered, betraying emotion thickening his tone. 'And to think—this was my last chance!'

Charlotte swayed towards him, and in a moment his arms were around her, his face buried in her neck. Now she could feel him trembling against her, and his vulnerability broke down all the barriers between them.

'Dear God, Charlotte,' he groaned, 'are you trying to kill me?'

'No. No.' Her arms slid round his waist, under his jacket, uncaring that other eyes were observing them now with avid interest. 'Oh, Logan, I'm sorry, I'm sorry.'

For a few moments he seemed unable to speak, and then at last, he drew back so that he could look into her face and she saw how pale he was. 'Why did you do it?' he demanded unsteadily. 'Why did you do it?'

Charlotte stroked back the hair from his forehead. 'How's Robert?' she asked huskily, and Logan closed his eyes for a moment in remembered agony.

'He's all right,' he said at last. 'Missing you like hell!'

'He—he didn't want to leave,' she stammered.

'Well, he sure as hell doesn't give that impression,' remarked Logan dryly. Then he glanced round. 'We can't stay here. I've got to speak to you alone. Do you have an hotel we could go to?'

'Do—do you?'

His eyes narrowed. 'Why? Don't you want me to know where you're staying?'

She shook her head. 'It's not that. It's—well, it's not very nice. I—I couldn't afford any better.'

'*Charlotte!*' The way he said her name made her knees go weak. 'All right, all right, we'll go to my hotel. It's not too far from here. So long as you trust me.'

Charlotte looked up at him adoringly. 'I don't need to trust you,' she said softly.

'For God's sake, don't look at me like that!' he muttered huskily, and taking her hand, dragged her after him towards the gates. It wasn't gentle, or particularly polite, but Charlotte loved it. Logan had hold of her hand, and so far as she was concerned, he could pull her through the very gates of hell and she would not object.

The hotel he was staying in was the same hotel he had used all those years ago when he was at the university. He saw her eyes dart up to take in the sign, and nodded half aggressively. 'It was the only place I knew. Do you mind?'

'Mind?' She shook her head, and with an exclamation he led her through the swinging doors and across the carpeted lobby.

His room was not the same. It was bigger for one thing, looking out across the park, and the bed was double instead of the narrow divan he slept on before. She preceded him into the room, and he closed the door behind them, securing the safety catch before turning towards her. She stood beside the bed, suddenly very aware of her pale cheeks and dark-ringed eyes, but Logan did not look at her. Instead, he remained where he was, saying quietly: 'I have to have an answer. Why did you run out on me?'

Charlotte linked her fingers round her bag. 'I—you were going to marry Elaine——'

'I was *not* going to marry Elaine!' he snapped savagely. 'I asked you to marry me, if you remember, but you refused.'

'For Robert's sake.'

'Yes, for Robert's sake. But mostly for mine. God, Charlotte, can't you see what you do to me?'

She badly wanted to be in his arms, but there were things that had to be said first. Taking a deep breath, she said: 'I—I learned today that—that you tried to see me before—before you left England.'

Now it was Logan's turn to look amazed. 'You—*what*?'

'I—I learned today——'

'Oh, yes, yes, I heard that. What do you mean by *today*?'

'What I say.' Charlotte took a step towards him. 'Logan, you've got to believe me. I didn't know!'

'You didn't know?' Logan stared at her aghast.

'I didn't. Matthew—Matthew never told me.'

'But my letters ...'

'I never got them. Matthew must have returned them himself.'

'I can't believe it.'

'You've got to believe it. It's the truth. As God is my witness, Logan, I am not lying to you.'

He raked back his hair, trying to make sense of what she was saying. 'You mean—you mean you weren't—*disgusted* by what had happened? You—you never said you didn't want to see me again?'

'No, no! That's what I'm telling you.' Charlotte wrung the strap of her bag. 'I—I've been talking to Dr Mannering. He—he told me what Matthew had said. I knew nothing of that. Logan, I—I loved you—I still love you!'

He looked absolutely stunned. 'You mean—all these years ...' He shook his head. 'Oh, my God! how could he do such a thing?'

'I don't know. Perhaps it was because of my mother. He wanted her once, but she loved my father. Then ... then the war came ...'

'And Matthew was made impotent,' finished Logan harshly. Then, at her surprised gasp, he added: 'I went to see his brother yesterday. I had the faint hope that you might have contacted them—that they might know where you were. When they learned who I was, they very quickly

184

let me know that poor dear Matthew couldn't possibly be the father of your son.'

Charlotte bent her head. 'When—when did you come to England?'

'Four days ago.' Logan looked at her now. 'As soon as I got back and found you'd gone.'

'Oh, Logan ...'

He covered the space between them in two strides, pulling at his tie impatiently. 'What did you think to achieve?'

'I—I didn't know about—about what happened—eleven years ago. I thought——'

'Yes?' he demanded. 'What did you think?' He made an impatient gesture. 'For God's sake, why do you think I brought you to the island? I didn't know Robert was my son then, did I?'

She shook her head. 'I—I thought you wanted to hurt me——'

'I did. I do.' His eyes swept down her slender body. 'But I know I'll only hurt myself more. Tell me something, how did you really feel after ... after ...'

'After we made love?' She lifted her face to his. 'You know how I felt.'

He swore softly. 'That call came in from the principal's office. You were crying ...'

'Aren't girls supposed to cry? I suppose I was young and frightened ...'

His hand caressed her cheek. 'With good cause, as it happened. I wonder if you'll get pregnant as quickly this time.'

'Logan!'

'Well!' He was unashamed. 'You are going to marry me, aren't you?'

Charlotte trembled. 'If you want me to.'

'If I want you to!' He raised his eyes heavenward for a moment. Then his hands dropped to the buttons of her shirt, making her tremble even more. 'Do you know what I did?' She shook her head, and he went on: 'After I got no joy out of ringing you and trying to see you and writing

185

letters to you, I went back to Rio. I thought—what the hell! The lady doesn't want to know. Forget her! But I couldn't. I loved you then as I love you now.' Her blouse came loose, and he pulled a face at the bra beneath. 'So I came back to London.' His hands slid round her back, seeking the clip that kept the bra in place. 'And when I found you had married Matthew, that you were pregnant, I actually tried to think of ways of killing you, do you know that?'

'Oh, Logan!'

The bra was loose, and he pushed it aside, bending his head to caress her hardening nipples with his lips. He was trembling now, she could feel it, and his eyes were dark and disturbingly sensual.

'But,' he continued speaking with evident difficulty, 'I knew that killing you I'd achieve nothing, only my own damnation, so I made other plans. It occurred to me that because Matthew was so much older than you were, sooner or later you were bound to be free, and when you were ...' He looked into her face deeply. 'I knew that somehow I would make you come to me. As it happened, it was easier than even I had imagined.'

'That—that was how Mr Lewis——'

'—learned about the post? Yes, of course. I explained that I was an old friend of Matthew's, who wanted to remain anonymous, etc., etc. He swallowed it without question. So, my sweet, did you.'

Charlotte's tongue appeared to wet her upper lip. 'And—and Robert?'

'Oh, yes, Robert.' He had unbuttoned his shirt now and was pulling her closer, his hair-roughened skin tickling her breasts. 'I hurt you. I'm sorry.' His tongue trailed a distracting path along her ear. 'That was why I slapped you, of course. When I saw him ...' He shook his head. 'Can you ever forgive me?'

'Can you forgive me?' she breathed, her lips turning against his cheek.

His eyes kindled with emotion. 'Only if you'll promise

to marry me, as soon as we can get a licence, here or in San Cristobal.'

'What about Elaine?'

'What about Elaine?' he asked impatiently, his mouth doing disturbing things to her powers of reasoning.

'Lisette told me—about Senhor Mendoza's plans for you. Your work at the Institute ...'

Logan sighed, loath to talk about such mundane things. 'All right,' he nodded. 'Manoel did hope that one day Elaine and I ...' He paused. 'He should have known better. No one buys my love and affection. It's not for sale. And Manoel is sufficiently much of a business man, I think, to overlook my deficiencies in that direction.'

Charlotte relaxed. 'It's all too good to be true.' Then her eyes clouded: 'But Robert——'

'What about him?'

'He's still in San Cristobal?'

'Yes. He's staying with Carlos. You don't have to worry, he's quite safe.'

'I'm not worried, but I am apprehensive.'

Logan frowned. 'What about?'

'Telling him.'

Now it was Logan's turn to be concerned. 'Oh, my darling, I have a confession to make ...'

Her lips trembled. 'What?'

'I—Robert knows already. I told him. You left me no alternative.'

Charlotte quivered. 'What did he say?'

'What did you expect him to say?' Logan half smiled. 'He said I needn't think he wanted a father who hurt his mother and sent her away!'

'Oh, Logan ...' She guessed how much it must have cost him to tell her that. 'He doesn't mean it.' She shook her head. 'Do you think he'll ever understand?'

Logan's fingers caressed her nape. 'When he's older perhaps. Right now, Carlos is doing a great job of public relations. And once we're married, and he has brothers and sisters ...'

187

'Brothers *and* sisters?' echoed Charlotte huskily. 'Aren't you being rather ambitious?'

'I don't think so,' remarked Logan, drawing her down on to the bed. 'And to begin ...'

What the press says about Harlequin romance fiction...

"When it comes to romantic novels... Harlequin is the indisputable king."
—*New York Times*

'Harlequin [is]... the best and the biggest.'"
—*Associated Press* (quoting Janet Dailey's husband, Bill)

"The most popular reading matter of American women today."
—*Detroit News*

"... exciting escapism, easy reading, interesting characters and, always, a happy ending.... They are hard to put down."
—*Transcript-Telegram*, Holyoke (Mass.)

"... a work of art."
—*Globe & Mail*, Toronto

What the press says about Harlequin romance fiction...

"When it comes to romantic novels...
Harlequin is the indisputable king."
  —*New York Times*

"...exciting escapism, easy reading, interesting
characters and, always, a happy ending....
They are hard to put down."
  — *Transcript-Telegram,* Holyoke (Mass.)

"...always...an upbeat, happy ending."
  —*San Francisco Chronicle*

"...a work of art."
  — *Globe & Mail,* Toronto

"Nothing quite like it has happened since
Gone With the Wind..."
  —*Los Angeles Times*

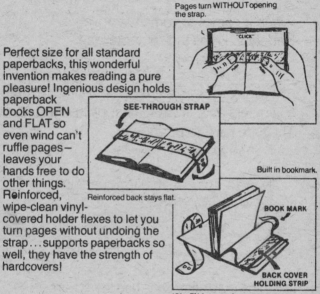